THE PORT

A VULNERABLE POINT FOR THE NEXT TERRORIST ATTACK

Victor Guembes, *CHS*

2009

First Edition

Designed by Victor Guembes
Templates prepared by Lulu Publishing
www.lulu.com

182,558 characters
417 KB

Lulu ID: 2648414

ISBN: 978-0-578-00546-1

Printed in the United States of America
Copyright © by Victor Guembes, *CHS*
2009

More than seven years have passed since the terrorist attacks
of September 11, 2001, events that changed the history
of the United States of America.
Billions of dollars have been allocated to the new
Department of Homeland Security in order to keep up
with the demanding development of new strategies
to be better prepared in detecting threats and
to counter attack the coward forces of evil.
The government has locked all doors but it keeps
ignoring that one of our windows still a vulnerable point
for a future disastrous attack:

THE PORT

THE PORT is a self-published book by Victor Guembes, *CHS*.
All opinions and matters discussed are the sole responsibility of the author unless statistics, references, or articles used as a reference for which clear indication of it has been made. The author apologizes in advance for any typing or grammar error during the work of this book.

The Port, Victor Guembes, *CHS*, printed in the USA, 2009

This book is dedicated to the men and women of the
United States Armed Forces and the Israeli Defense Forces (IDF)
for their remarkable fight against terrorism.

Also to:

Saymar and Katrina, two wonderful girls in my life.

Get Ready........!

INDEX

Afghanistan
"The Initiation Phase"
-9-

Iran
"The Training Phase"
-31-

Tampa, Florida, USA
"Testing the Waters"
-51-

Afghanistan
"Regrouping"
-71-

Tampa, Florida, USA
"The Execution Plan"
-85-

The Kaljatahl Triumph
-113-

"The epoch of adhering to Western prescriptions has passed. The enemies of Islam are seeking to separate religion from politics. Using seductive Western concepts such as political parties, competitive pluralist political systems and bogus democracy, the Westernized are trying to present a utopic picture of Western societies and portray them as the only salvation for our Islamic society".

Seyed Ali Khamenei
Iran, July 24, 1998

The Port, USA, 2009

AFGHANISTAN
"The Initiation Phase"

The beat up white Mercedes was going East on Falahl al-Dinar Avenue in Kabul and it seemed that it would stop before it gets to the only service station that operates until 8 pm. At the wheel, Kadu didn't think twice and stopped the vehicle to thank the Almighty for the safe return of his brother Hassan from London after his participation in a bombing incident at Lancaster University.

Kadu continued driving and pulled in the driveway of the service station where a tall, skinny man greeted him like if he was the only customer of the day. Kadu requested a quick oil change on his way to use the restroom and the old man drove the vehicle in for the service requested. The loneliness and coldness of a deserted area covered the shop where the noises of an upcoming sand storm mixed in the air with the ones coming from the old tools used for the Mercedes' service were the choir for what was imminent to happen. Kadu was thankful for the safe return of his brother who stayed at home on the West side of the city, but very disappointed to learn that the old man tried to cash a reward for tipping the allied forces led by the American troops about a suspicion he had of Hassan's involvement in the alleged attack in the English nation. No more than four minutes were necessary to tape the bomb on the pipes under the sink before Kadu started a conversation with the old man who was struggling to remove the used oil filter. There was no inquietude to know why the old man reported his suspicions to the allied forces regarding Hassan's involvement in the bombing at the University, nor there was questioning about the London incident. It just didn't matter. After the job was done, Kadu with a sarcastic smile, but with the firm conviction that the sand storm would erase part of the town for a few weeks, decided to tap the old man on the shoulder, got in the white Mercedes and slowly drove away, like wanted to just look at the service station for the last time. He drove towards the West. The old man put away the cash and lighted up a nasty tiny roll of tobacco while contemplating a starving dog near the dumpster outside the shop searching for food. Less than quarter of a mile, Kadu grabbed his cell phone and dialed the number of victory, but there was no answer; just an explosion. The service station blew up in thousands of pieces through the air and the old man and his dog were just unaware of the successes and died immediately after as a consequence of the blast. The white Mercedes did not change direction and it continued going to the West at least for forty minutes.

Kadu was about 30 miles to the West from the scene of the rubble, but did not escape the storm already predicted for the entire region. He had no other choice than going home, relax and to watch the news on his black and white Zenith. The news didn't came until ten o'clock at night, only four hours after the attack, and this was a fast broadcast compared to other incidents.

The allied forces were in charge of the investigation and the local police under the command of Captain Manzar Hajak, an Afghan who wanted a change in the nation's future, sealed the surroundings for the upcoming investigation.

Captain Hajak was immune to the pain and to any shock with respect to the bloody evidences. He was always committed to the reconstruction process of Afghanistan and very eager in learning as much as possible from the masters of freedom. A few people gathered at the scene of the terrorist attack and children were playing close by, but paying more attention to the soccer game on an imaginary field just a few blocks away. The officer in charge of the investigation for the Allied Command was Major Lee Hegedus, who ordered the lifting of evidences after the photographs were taken and asked to be sent to the New Hampshire military compound in the rocky mountains of the northeast side of Kabul. It was routine, and it seemed like the attack didn't bother Major Hegedus much, who left the scene after twenty minutes heading back to the compound to continue the briefly suspended domino tournament.

On the other side of town and inside a modest house, Kadu and Hassan were reunited and joined the party giving by their parents for the successful accomplishment of the London incident. It was not easy to survive undetected while living on campus at Lancaster University, but it was a moment of joy and prayers. Both brothers knew about the incident that just happened on the other side of town and their ties were more than familiar, more than blood, more than religious, it was a matter of commitment to the initiation of an enormous, tedious and complicated plan, the commitment to harm the United States whenever the opportunity arises in the future. The prayers were said and all the venerations concluded; it was time for food. One table and three non-matching chairs was the epicenter of the starting point of the big plan. The parents and friends didn't have any knowledge of what was in Kadu's mind, the instigator and mastermind of the plan, and they could never believe of the tenacity and balls of Hassan to carry on with the plan, as he was appointed as one of the possible multiple executors of an unknown plan. The plan was not designed yet; it was only a desire and a commitment for the future.

Several men were drinking and eating in the living room, while the women and children were playing in the backyard, the music was typical and instrumental, and it was getting close to midnight. They had only two more hours before the curfew surprise them in their way home and the metallic noise of the allied forces tanks were getting in position as they have been doing it for the past several months. The broadcast of the attack called the attention of the women first, since the only television set was in the master bedroom and one of them shout for her husband to watch the sinister report. All men, including Kadu and Hassan expressed their condolence and elevated their prayers to the Almighty for the prompt political change of the nation. Captain Hajak served as the spoke person for the security forces to the Jamalali Television informing of possible clues left by the perpetrator. He was trying to comfort the population, and Kadu knew better that there was no evidence left at the scene. The women started to prepare small packages with food to take home and they were leaving all at once. Kadu went to his room and started to brainstorm a morbid plan while Hassan stayed in the living room to sleep on the couch as he did it every night. Minutes after 2 am, the tense noise of the armored vehicles was the only melody played to the population until the sunrise.

There was something that was bothering Kadu's pride and mind and it was the announcement made by Captain Hajak during the television interview, somebody who he considered a traitor. Hajak was born in 1970 in the northern region of Afghanistan, raised in France until his fifteenth birthday during his father's assignment to the Medical Research Center for Contemporary Viruses in the French capital; then he joined the Paul Levoir Military Academy in Paris. In 1995, he entered the United States as member of a medical research group and settled in the city of Brandon, near Tampa in Florida. In 1998 he moved to London where he took some courses at Lancaster University. Finally, in May of 2004 he went back to Afghanistan and joined the new reformed police force trained by the allied forces, mainly directed by the United States of America. What Kadu didn't know was that Captain Hajak was infiltrated to the new force to gather information on any matter pertaining to the reconstruction of the Afghan government. His previous preparation and education gave him the opportunity to keep a high ranking position and direct participation in meetings with the allied forces.

What Hajak didn't know is that somewhere in town a man by the name of Kadu was thinking to prepare a plan to assassinate him because this man considered him a traitor to their faith and religion as well as to their political objectives. Kadu promptly started to locate the substation where Captain Hajak was working and started to observe the normal routine of its members, the police compound, its security, the parking lot, the routes of escape, and everything in the surroundings. One morning, about 6 am just a few minutes after the sunrise, Kadu was in the rear seat of the old Mercedes Benz, which was parked about two blocks from the police compound and spotted a lunch wagon nearby frequented by armed policemen zipping hot chocolate and hot tea. He got out of the car and walked slowly towards the lunch wagon and when approaching it he asked for a cup of hot tea. He had a conversation with many policemen and seemed interested in the reconstruction of a new Afghanistan. He just blended himself with the crowd and made some positive comments about Captain Hajak's presentation on television. One of the policemen, wearing an American fatigue pair of pants, a light blue shirt two sizes more of what he was supposed to wear to look professional, made a comment that Captain Hajak should be out soon to have his cup of tea and that if Kadu wants to meet him he should not go away. Kadu couldn't believe that he was close to meet with a traitor. An American serviceman with a M16 on his left shoulder was approaching the lunch wagon and by his side a dark skin man with an uneven mustache and a sweaty light blue shirt and yawning while walking fast to get the daily cup of tea met Kadu who seemed impressed and saluted the pair.

Kadu told Hajak that he looked the same in person as on television and that he was grateful that the new Afghanistan was in process thanks to the courage of outer armies and internal police forces coalition. Hajak smiled and simply thanked him for his comments and proceeded to his first zip of hot tea. Kadu insisted and thanked him again, but this time he mentioned to Hajak that unfortunately many citizens are not happy and do not share the matter of having allied troops led by the American government inside Afghanistan and that he must be careful with the opposition. Hajak simply responded: "Do not worry my friend. I have lived in this nation for over thirty eight years and I am planning for thirty eight more, and the only way to reach that is by fixing today what is wrong and what is in the way to prevent it". Kadu finished the cup of tea and walked away to his vehicle while Hajak observing him, had the small feeling that Kadu wanted to talk more about issues that may be in common. Half way to his car Kadu heard the cranky voice of the dark skin man who asked him to stop. Hajak told him on his native dialect: "Your eyes don't match the feelings from your heart". And Kadu responded: "Your feelings do not match what you said on television". Hajak, a little intense tried to stimulate Kadu to think about a new nation under new rules for a better future, but Kadu abruptly told him not to continue in an unwanted process of reconstruction and to think about his thirty eight years in Afghanistan and that the only way he will make thirty eight more is by preserving what the American troops were trying to destroy, their dignity. Hajak invited Kadu for more tea, but this time at his place three days later and after the sunset. Kadu went home and the dust and smoke expelled from the old Mercedes covered the rearview mirror to the point that only tiny parts of Hajak's body were visible.

Kadu went home and spoke with his brother Hassan letting him know that an imminent and great opportunity has arrived, and the chance to eliminate Hajak was clearly easy and necessary. What Hassan and Kadu didn't know is that the short legged Captain wanted to leave the force and join a combatant cell with broad ramifications all the way from the rocky- mountains of Afghanistan to the sunny city of Tampa in Florida, all the way in the United States.

Hassan pulled a dirty pillow case from under the old couch in the hallway between his room and the dark living room. Parts of an AK-47 were soaked in oil and it was time to clean them and put the rifle back together. Both brothers had the commitment to annihilate Hajak considered a traitor to the cause of the Afghan population and their interests.

Back on the East side of town, the bombing of the service station didn't bother anyone anymore; it was just another unresolved mystery and an unwanted case to be preoccupied for. The night of the encounter was close, only hours was separating the supposedly traitor and the rebel brothers.

Inside the trunk of the old Mercedes there was a bottle of British cognac, a box of dark chocolates, a can of American peanuts, and four warm cans of American beer mixed with hundreds of rounds for the AK-47. The plan was that Hassan will be driving while Kadu with a handgun will just walk to the door and fire to kill Hajak at the doorsteps. They were not interested in the cup of tea and in no conversation. However, Hajak was not home when the buzzer sounded, two men answered the door and asked Kadu to come in. Hassan was also called to join them and both went inside the modest house.

The brothers sat near the backyard, were food and drinks were notorious over a small table; there was no tea. Captain Hajak showed up after parking the American hummer issued to him behind the Mercedes. While inside, Hajak told the men that Afghanistan has a different mission for him in order to rescue and to fight for the future of the nation. The strong odor of alcohol invaded the backyard before the two brothers were able to say anything. The men that opened the door raise their glasses and cheers for the initiation of a new partnership. Kadu did not understand the moment. He was confused and astonished that Hajak was able to read his heart when having a cup of tea near the police station a few days ago.

My brother, stated Hajak while looking to Kadu's eyes, there is no form to thank the Almighty for the enormous day when we met. There is something typically mystic in the way Afghan people tie their efforts to destroy their enemies. Hassan was very confused also and took the initiative to ask: Is this a meeting between citizens and police forces or a meeting between the sons of the Almighty for a cause? One of the men who answered the door stated: This is more than a meeting; this is the meeting of victory where our hearts are and will be the driving force to destroy the enemy.

Hajak paused for ten seconds and proceeded to explain. Nobody at that meeting was able to leave or to quit. They all were committed and decisive to create a plan, something big, and something effective and powerful. Drinks were spilled all over the floor and food was enough for a battalion while the soft music emphasizes the rhythm of an upcoming event.

The night went by and Hajak was telling many stories of how and why he enrolled in the police force. It was opportunity and necessity, the food and training was good, the pay was excellent and his father was taken care of at an American medical tent to treat his emphysema. Kadu explained his ambition to travel to the United States to make it shake; Hassan stated that he wanted to bring every big building down in the major cities in America, and the two unknown men stated that they wanted to kill traitors or false individuals who just wanted an opportunity. The brothers looked at each other and with a smile looked back to the men and Hajak, and stated that they also wanted to kill traitors. More drinks were spilled as they were losing control of their glasses filled with the English cognac.

Hajak, mentioned that he was able to travel to the United States with no problems and that he used to live in the city of Tampa, Florida while attending college classes and medical conventions.

He has many contacts in Tampa, people who worked in different hemispheres and knew their way around. Before anything was initiated, Hajak explained, they have to meet with Sheik Lazur almad Al Fanistar, a clergyman in the town of Kastan who is considered one of the masterminds and heavy men in politics for the new era in Afghanistan. Sheik Al Fanistar had too many contacts in New York, Chicago, Los Angeles, Kansas, and Tampa.

Sometime in July of 2004, Kadu, Hassan, Hajak and his two friends Mardak and Wadek met at the Sheik's house near the town of Kastan. Before the meeting, maybe a few hours before, Hajak passed by the police station and informed Major Hegedus that he will be out of town for three to four days due to a family emergency in the town of Lemeuth, a town on the opposite side of Kastan.

Kadu and Hassan were having dinner at their place and were talking about the previous encounter with Hajak at his house. Hassan looked eager to continue and to give everything for the cause against the imperialism injected in the region by the American forces and the government.

Kadu was willing to carry on with any lethal operation for the same cause and he trusted the charisma of the Sheik and the goals of Hajak and his men to plan an operation against the United States.

Kastan was about two hours north and the Mercedes made it perfectly. The two brothers were twenty minutes late, but it was not a big deal. They only missed the first round of British cognac. At the Sheik's place, a rectangular wooden table was the center of negotiation and planning of the objective. On top of the table, there were two pots of hot tea, a plate with dried fruit and nuts, several pieces of bread, cognac, pipes and tobacco. Hajak did have a plan and now he had the right people for the plan and started to expose it to the audience. His plan was to travel to the United States, settle for a while in the city of Tampa, meet with the rest of the team at the port of Tampa who they were to arrive on a Greek ship and execute the bombing of several oil and gas reservoir tanks and destroy the entire port. He mentioned that the easiest location to conduct the plan was Tampa because his familiarization with the place, his contacts in India with members of the Al-Yamat terrorist group that were dominating the port operations in the region and were hired as crewmen for different companies around the world. Hajak knew the vulnerable points at the port and about the lack of security in it, and because the strategic point to conduct the operation. Everybody agreed, but still no clear plan. It seemed impossible and it may take too long to put everything together. Hajak just wanted it that way; it was a done deal and the next step was to contact the members of Al-Yamat through some of his followers stationed in Afghanistan.

The night was getting close and the members of the meeting were almost intoxicated and full of ideas and great-spirit. They finished the meeting praying to the Almighty for the success of their future plan that just started.

Hajak went back to the police station where Major Hegedus informed him that he should be preparing for the upcoming visit of Mr. Karl Blastorm, the senior advisor for security operations for the President of the United States. Major Hegedus appointed Captain Hajak as the main liaison between the bodyguards of the official to come and the Afghan forces. It was an annual meeting and the last one prior to the presidential elections in Kabul.

On the other side of town, the two brothers were celebrating the news that they will be part of history and part of the few good men and heroes chosen to participate in a spiritual plan.

For the next few weeks Hajak was training dozens of paramilitary troops that would be in charge of the security task force of Mr. Blastorm. Near the University of Kabul, signs were posted announcing the meeting between the American envoy and the two presidential candidates at the Jamalali television station. Not everybody would be able to watch the debate and meeting on television unless, all neighbors get together in somebody's house that possesses a television set. That was not important for the coalition forces; the main objective was to set up precedents that a meeting was in place and that the election process was taking care of by following certain steps within the diplomatic relations between the Afghan government and the coalition forces interested in the reconstruction of the new nation.

Mr. Blastorm was scheduled to arrive on the morning of the first Monday of July, 2004. The preparation for elections was imminent and it was of an enormous interest for the American government to get it over soon, and to place the pre-assigned candidate as the new democratic president of Afghanistan, Mr.

Fakeq Ramad, a long time economist graduated from the University of London, and a long time resident of that city. Mr. Ramad was an admirer of the economical and political system typically of imperialist nations and seems to be very eager to convert Afghanistan into a competitive market for the world. He was under the microscope for many years by the British and he seemed the perfect candidate to support upon his return to his native place and to provide him with the most sophisticated security while in power as the new president of Afghanistan. However, the second candidate, Mr. Rayid Torjal was very close to the imperialist system, he knew way ahead that his participation was only to have a competitor and that his short term participation will end up with the victory of Ramad. Captain Hajak met with Major Hegedus the night before the arrival to expose his contingency plan for the security of the American official.

Everything was meticulously prepared and analyzed; the roadblocks were in place and the barricades with Afghan snipers ready to pull the trigger to unannounced persons in the area. Major Hegedus was leading the coalition security forces for the event and had a perfect communication with Hajak to fulfill a job well done from the airport to the sets of Jamalali television.

While the preparation was happening, Kadu and his brother Hassan were at home positioning the improvised antenna of the black and white Zenith to watch the arrival and debate of the two candidates presided by the Senior Advisor coming from the United States and some other officials of the new Afghan Congress. They knew it was a prepared circus and that everything was faked to show up to the world the efficient way to create new democratic governments and to justify the invasion of a supposed nation in need of it.

The anger and hatred for the imperialism just gained weight and their desires to carry on with a terrorist plan in the same United States was even greater. They watched the entire debate just to feed the soul to attack the American soil with patriotism. They just didn't know how long it will take from the planning phase to the execution phase; this matter was left to Captain Hajak who was ready to quit the police force and to dedicate his time to the new adventure.

Major Hegedus always counted with the support and the job well done from Captain Hajak, but some rumors were already spread that this Afghan officer was ready to leave the force. Two days after the departure of the American official, Major Hegedus called Captain Hajak to his office for a meeting. The conversation was kind of tense, but friendly and Hegedus couldn't resist to go around the bushes and asked Hajak directly: "I heard you are planning to leave the force, is that true?" Captain Hajak, who was sitting on a comfortable chair with arm rests and padded back support with Iranian fabric jumped from it and gave a few steps forward without saying a word.
Hegedus was calm and followed Hajak's steps with his blue eyes. Hajak took a breath and slowly but firmly answered: "I have to do it. I did my part and I did it well. Now is time for me to carry on with my personal business". Hegedus offered him more training or money and he even asked what else was needed for him to stay. Hajak responded: "All I want is to take care of my family and give the opportunity to other citizens to take charge. Hegedus replied: "If you want, I can arrange a meeting with Colonel Staples, the head of the coalition forces at the Alpha quadrant of the region, and maybe something better and more adequate comes up for you.....remember we all are working for a new Afghanistan and you should be excited and willing to have direct participation in

it". Hajak walked back to his seat and rested his chin over his right hand and slowly replied: "Major Hegedus, I'm very grateful for the entire support I received from you and from the coalition forces. But, there is something in me that is not allowing me to continue and I must take care of.....in a way it will also contribute to the fight we are fighting". Hegedus was confused and tried to understand. He blinked his eyes over and over and walked to the side table were the bottle of cognac started to shake after his firm steps rumbled the wooden floor. Would you like a glass? He asked to Hajak, who replied with a head movement as a negative. Hegedus had the drink anyway and asked Hajak to think over again and to come back to him the next day. Hajak had in mind to come back again, but had to re-schedule his meeting with the Sheik since he did not want to be absent-without-leave (AWOL).

Hajak left the room and went back to the barracks to retrieve the keys of the hummer; he knew it would be one of his last rides with it. At home, he called his team mates Wadek and Mardak for dinner but omitted to call Hassan and Kadu; he just wanted to make some slightly changes in the beginning phase of the enormous and important plan. At dinner time, the three men were reunited and attentive to the plan. Hajak informed them that they needed to go to Kastan and meet with Sheik Lazur almad Al Fanistar and informed him that the meeting for his blessing had to be postpone one more day, and to stay in Kastan just waiting for him. He also asked the men to stop by Kadu's house to let them know to leave the same night to Kastan and to wait for him at the stand of flowers at the market in Kastan and to wait to be picked up.

The next morning, Hajak met with Colonel Staples, a rude and build up officer with the American troops and head of the Alpha quadrant in the region. A Marine all the way, made sound his tone of voice with sweetness and direct his first statement to Major Hegedus: "So, this man is Captain Hajak, ah!" Yes Sir, responded Hegedus. Staples extended his right hand and made Hajak feel more comfortable. Hajak stated: "Yes Sir, I am the one". Major Hegedus helped himself with a glass of British cognac; it seemed that he was getting ready for a tough meeting. However, Colonel Staples without asking why Captain Hajak wanted out simply stated: "I am the type of guy who never get involved in people's personal agenda. I like to help and to do everything within my power to change things and to make people more comfortable". He continued, is there anything I can do for you to stay, Captain Hajak? The Captain looked to his left and he was amazed of the big zip of cognac Major Hegedus just swallowed, turned back his head to the Colonel and said: "No, Sir. I just wanted out and I wish you all the best. I have to take care of my family, and I want to do it right". Staples simply directed his eyes to Major Hegedus and said: "Major, take Captain Hajak to your office and bring me back the papers for his release". He also stated with a sarcastic smile looking at Hajak: "You are lucky, things here are done different than in the States, to get out is a process; here is just a decision". Good luck to you! Major Hegedus saluted the Colonel and asked permission to leave the room. Captain Hajak forgot the salute because he was astonished of what just happened. They both left en route to Hegedus' office.

It was around 3 pm, Mardak and Wadek were already at the Sheik's place enjoying some fruit platters and prayers along the afternoon. Kadu and Hassan were arriving at the market and they were enjoying it, but they noticed that there were not too many locals; instead, there were a lot of servicemen from the coalition forces getting drunk, and playing games never played in the country before.

Around 4 pm, Captain Hajak officially signed his resignation from the police force at the military compound. Just a few members of the coalition forces gave him the salute. This was the last time he saw the flags of Britain, the United States, Honduras, Australia, Spain, Canada, Kuwait, and Germany together at the same military compound. The keys of the hummer were turned in. Hajak jumped in the old motorcycle parked for months at the compound and drove away en route to his house.

At his place, Hajak grabbed the already packed backpack, some cigarettes and continue to Kastan, just two hours apart. He made it to the market around 7 pm, just an hour before its closing time, but couldn't find Kadu and Hassan. They both were inside the brothel a few steps from the flower stand. Hajak found the men and shared some cigarettes and were en route to the Sheik's place. The Mercedes was following the noisy motorcycle. Fifteen minutes later, they drove over a dirt path left by Wadek and Mardak when en route to the extended field to reach the Sheik's cabin. Already at the place, they were all greeted and prayers were said. There was some food left over, like pieces of bread, fresh fruit and some tea. The new guests ate all, one because the trip was long, and the brothers because they had too much activity at the brothel.

Sheik Lazur almad Al Fanistar arranged some improvised beds for the five men along the cabin providing them with some blankets, pillows, candles, and a big pot of tea. They stayed up together until 10 pm just praying for the encounter to be blessed and to ask for a productive morning, a new day where all the steps of the new plan will take place.

The next morning Major Hegedus found a copy of the book *The Lion's Cancer* at the barracks, a book he gave to Hajak to practice his English and to read about matters in terrorism. This was a reason to see Hajak again, and Major Hegedus took the book and secured it in his office having in mind to see Hajak a week later during his free time.

The sun came up around 6 am, the Sheik was already up and he was preparing fresh tea and baking fresh bread in the brick oven. The guests were up one by one and got together for the daily prayers before they sat at the improvised extended table. There were six men at the table, the Sheik, Kadu, Hassan, Hajak, Mardak, and Wadek. The spiritual leader and mastermind of the entire plan initiated the meeting with additional prayers in the name of the Almighty. The guests were anxious to learn about their role in the plan, but also they were eating the fresh bread soaked in fresh tea.

The Sheik started to explain. The plan was to carry on an attack to one of the most vulnerable ports in the United States, the Port of Tampa. The information was previously provided to the Sheik by elements currently living and working in the city of Tampa after an exhaustive surveillance looking and assessing vulnerable points. However, the new measures adopted by the United States government in regards of homeland security made some steps of the plan difficult but not impossible. It may require additional time and more precautions, but the window of opportunity was still wide for infiltrations and sacred operations as they seemed to consider.

The Sheik wanted Hajak to travel to Tampa and to meet with some contacts since he was previously living in the United States and because he would get a visa under the conditions of his previous service with the new reformed police force under the mandate of the coalition forces. He spoke English and he was very smart and impulsive to carry on with the plan as he would be the right man to be in charge of the operation while in the States under the spiritual command of the Sheik. Hassan, Kadu, Mardak and Wadek were to be arriving aboard a Greek vessel transporting cement to an American-Greek company stationed at the Port of Tampa, and for which they were to be hired for that mission at the port of Harachi in India. The business of hiring ship workers was run by members of the Al-Yamat terrorist organization, publicly known as one of the most efficient marine operators. Hajak was to depart to Tampa no later than the last day of September 2004 and to be involved in surveillance and re-adaptation process until the last day of January 2005. By then Hajak, will communicate with the Sheik for an update of the initiation phase of the plan. The other combatants will travel to Iran and meet with members of the Al-Yamat terrorist organization for training; if they pass the training they will go to India as already hired workers to work at the port of Harachi.

All these steps were to be done by the end of January 2005 also. If the plan goes as established, reports to the Sheik will come from Tampa and Harachi to connect the men and proceed with the following steps.
In the meantime, members of the Islamic fundamentalist community in Tampa were alerted and were preparing to carry on with the supportive plan designed as a strategy to provide all the necessary support and information step by step for the upcoming sacred event.
After the Sheik exposed the plan to the combatants, comments were obvious and expected. Hajak took the lead and stated: "This is something I was waiting all my life, and I have lived enough to

know the Almighty and to enjoy his words during my childhood, adolescence and maturity. Now is time for me to offer to the Almighty the power I have to destroy the evil forces of the Americans that with their imperialism and evil habits have willingly destroyed and embarrassed the Muslim world". Kadu and Hassan stand up followed by Mardak and Wadek and hugged each other whispering the name of Ala over an over. The Sheik slowly grabbed the warm cup of tea and cheers with the combatants.

A few days later, Hassan and Kadu were enjoying dinner with their family and they knew they would be missing the goat cheese and fresh bread made by their parents. Hassan told his brother that what happened month ago at the Lancaster University was nothing in comparison to what is going to be when they carry on a successful plan in the United States.

Hajak was covering his motorcycle parked at the rear of his modest house and a noise over the dry leaves made him turn around to found a dirty pair of boots, very familiar to him, wore by Major Hegedus who came to look for him. Hajak was surprised to see him again and asked him to come in for a drink. This was not the time to be cheering with Americans anymore, but Hajak didn't have any other choice in order to avoid suspicions. However, Major Hegedus asked him: "Are you planning to leave town?" And Hajak responded: "You said that because I covered my motorcycle? Not really. I am going to visit my parents who live at the other side of the Kardastan mountains and I won't be back maybe for a couple of months from now".

Major Hegedus reached for his bag hanging on his right shoulder and handled him the book left at the barracks and saying: "Hey my friend, you may need this for the long journey". Hajak with a smile replied: "Thanks Major, I sure will need it", and placed the book on the table. They had tea and dried fruit together. Hajak learned from Major Hegedus that his wife is about to have a newborn two months later and that he may be going back to the States for a while. Hajak said: "All I know is the State of Florida you know, I used to live there before". Hegedus replied: "I know that. But, I'm from Pennsylvania which is located northeast and far from Florida". The meeting was over and Major Hegedus departed after they share another cup of tea and a big hug.

Sheik Lazur almad Al Fanistar had the passport, flight ticket and required transportation to the Kabul airport for Hajak. A small linen bag containing one thousand American dollars was also ready. Hajak was to depart later on in the week. The other combatants were also getting ready to depart to Iran for their training.
It was a cold Saturday morning and Hajak departed en route to Kastan to spend the night at the Sheik's cabin for a night of prayers. The night went by and Hajak had plenty rest waking up around 9 am on Sunday. A big breakfast and the last prayers in the name of the Almighty were said. One of the Sheik's assistants drove Hajak to Kabul's airport, a few hours of thinking, a few hours of prayers, and a few hours of ride went by like a day for Hajak. He did not have a chance to said goodbye to Kadu, Hassan, Mardak and Wadek. It was done on purpose by the Sheik; at this time they just followed orders from the clergyman.

The same day but late in the afternoon, the other four combatants were going on their own to Kabul's airport for their destination to Iran. Both teams, a one-man team and the four men team were in the direction the Sheik wanted and for a long waited caused, a necessary period of time after the September 11 attacks before another great attack is carried on.

The trip was short for the men traveling to Iran compared to Hajak's trip who was going first to London, then to New York, then to Atlanta, and finally to Tampa.

IRAN
"The Training Phase"

The white and blue shuttle bus with horizontal green stripes was the one designated to pick up the members of the Kaljatahl group. As named by the Sheik, the Kaljatahl group was en route to experience a rigorous training at an undisclosed camp somewhere south of Teheran.

The Iranian flight landed on time and the new trainees were already part of a team, but they didn't know it until the man in charge of their transportation and training, Mosur Q'alghi welcomed them and told them that right at that moment they were known as the Kaljatahl group. The shuttle bus had the door open and the engine running. A few meters behind a marked police vehicle with two officers heavily armed providing security to the bus, but without anybody else knowing of it. The armed guards were apparently providing security to the airfield strip where the plane landed. Inside the bus, a member of the Mujaedin terrorist organization provided security with an AK-47, two survival knives, and one additional Kalashnikov rifle on top of the back seat of the bus. The partial exposure of his face resembled the sanguinary look of a mercenary or terrorist. Kadu, Hassan, Mardak and Wadek got in the bus and enjoyed the ride. Mixed feelings and vibrations were invading their bodies and souls; there was no connection or communication with the Sheik or with Hajak, already en route to the United States. This is another isolated process of the training and of the makeup process of holy combatants.

It took over an hour before they stop seeing buildings and people and they were entering an isolated area with some small mountains, a desert-type location, dry and non-friendly atmosphere. They could almost smell the gunpowder and hear the shouts of the trainers; their lips were dry as if they were already running and denied water by the instructors; they knew the times of good sleep were over and that the parties of good food and cognac were part of history. They started to missed Hajak and the good moments together in Kabul. But, all of them were praying in the bus and getting the spiritual energy from the Almighty, and reading the scriptures of the holy Q'uoran as indicated by the Sheik.

The overheated bus made a suddenly stop at a checkpoint. A couple of heavily armed guards ordered everybody out of the bus. There were only seven people: Kadu, Hassan, Mardak, Wadek, two other unknown individuals and the security from the Mujaedins. The driver showed his identification to the guards and remained in the bus. The Mujaedin made contact with the guards and obtained the clear sign to enter the compound. This is the initiation of the next step during the preparatory phase of an upcoming event. The men got in the bus again. The ride was short. Only five minutes later the bus stopped at another checkpoint and slightly parked at the right side of it. The occupants were ordered to descend and to enter a cabin and to wait for further orders. The Kaljatahl group was surprised that the other two unknown males in the bus didn't enter the cabin; instead they were ordered to stay outside the cabin. These two unknown males for them were actually traitors to the Mujaedins that were ordered to go to the airport and to make the bus look occupied, but in fact the security guard in the bus had orders to shoot at them if they tried to run away. Now at the camp, the two unknown deserters were tied up on a pole waiting for their executors. A tall man with a grown beard, strong voice, sweaty, and smoking a long cigarette came inside the cabin an introduced himself as Alfad Dal Kaden, the chief of the boot camp.

Mosur Q'alghi, the chief instructor, told the new trainees in front of the chief that it was the beginning of hell to reach heaven by means of annihilating the enemy from its roots. Alfad Dal Kaden added to the statement: "Either you make it or you will be executed". The men raised their chests and were willing to fight for the cause. Q'alghi asked for two volunteers for a special task, and Kadu and Wadek took a step ahead, showing their enthusiasm and desires to start the training. They were given two survival type knives and they were ordered to go outside the cabin to kill both men that were tied up, the traitors. Kadu took the first steps, opened the door and choose for the one that used to be seated next to him on the bus introducing the weapon deep inside the traitor's throat claiming victory to Alah. Kadu's hands were soaked in blood and his breathing was controlled but deep, his sight was oriented and deep, and his spirit was joyful and eager to start the training. Wadek observed the coldness and prompt execution of the first traitor and he knew what was to come for him. He decided to put the knife deep in the other man's heart; he did it so hard that the blade almost bend but sure enough to feel the flesh and blood in his own hands. Both men died minutes later.

Alfad Dal Kaden had a task for Hassan and Mardak, maybe a little less extraordinary. They both knew they were tested by the chief and that they cannot step back. They were ordered to untie the bodies and transport them over their shoulders to the already prepared burning point. They both carried the dead bodies over to the next location and set them on fire. The Kaljatahl group just had their welcome party at the compound.

Alfad Dal Kaden released the men to Mosur Q'alghi who was in charge of the entire training and psychological preparation of the combatants. Q'alghi took the men to an improvised barracks with pieces of cartons over the dirt ground to be used as beds; he showed the men two holes on the ground to be used as toilets, and pointed at the big and old lavatory filled with water from a water-truck that passed by every morning if it didn't break down.

Q'alghi asked them to feel comfortable and to drop their bags near their beds. When they did that, dust covered their pillows made up of paper and fabric residues. The instructor told them that they have five prayers during the day and three meals. The so-called breakfast was served at 5am, a warm lunch around noon, and a good dinner around 6pm, just two hours prior to go to bed as a mandatory routine for the first week of training.

That night there was no dinner, and they all shared a big round piece of bread with one can of Russian sardines. It was tasteful, it was good, and it was enough. They went to bed by 8pm.

Around 4am, Q'alghi discharged about one hundred rounds from his AK-47 just millimeters from each combatant improvised bed on the ground as their wake-up call. They were up and muted. The water truck didn't arrived and they were ready for training without washing their faces. The Kaljatahl group joined several other combatants who were sleeping at a different location and who had also a different mission somewhere in the world. Nobody was allowed to know of each other's mission. They all knew they were fighters, freedom fighters against the American imperialism and committed to the destruction of Israel as well. Q'alghi took the group of about twenty combatants for a run. They were ordered to take off their shoes and socks and started the run on the dirt shouting phrases and songs from the holy book. They were far, they couldn't see the compound, and in their way back the formation was not the same, it seemed like a snake, and the head was Q'alghi.

At the compound the men met inside a circle enclosed by broken bricks and rocks, demarking the area were exercises were to be conducted. Push ups and sit ups were all they did until their muscles started to curl up and they started to roll in pain. Q'alghi could smell the fresh bread brought by carriage and stopped the training.

The group of combatants marched to an old tent. A round table sitting on top of a discolored American flag had bread, tea, goat cheese and fruit. As soon as they entered the tent, food was distributed for the hungry combatants who were having zips of hot tea. Just three minutes passed before the smell of tear gas invaded the entire tent and the sound of AK-47 rounds whistled the entrance of it, not permitting anybody to leave the tent, otherwise they would be reached by a bullet. The men hit the ground, and they were coughing badly. Q'alghi entered the tent wearing a gas mask with the inscriptions US by the nose filters; he ordered the men to leave the tent immediately. Breakfast was over.

In formation they had head count and proceeded to the classroom, another tent with holes as windows. A rectangular blackboard with Islamic scriptures on the far top right of it was the main décor of the main area of philosophical and psychological endurance. From that point on, the training consisted in the planning of a terrorist attack in general, the identification of routes of escape, survival techniques, evasion strategies, and the focus on resistance when dealing with the enemy forces anywhere in the world. Nothing was done without elevating a prayer to the Almighty first. For the next two months the training was constant, increasing in the difficulty of the tasks and of an enormous physical endurance. No men dropped; they were soldiers all the way for a cause.

After two months of training, the combatants were allowed to visit nearby towns and to visit religious places as a mandatory mission. To do so, a pick up truck of Russian fabrication was the only mean to transport them from the compound to Barsak, Almanei, or Hurdeksak, the three main nearby villages. They learned that in Almanei, there was a market where they were able to used cellular phones. The pickup truck was driven by Mardak, Kadu as a passenger in the front seat, and Hassan and Wadek on the cargo section reading an old Islamic newspaper left there with stains from who knows what. On their first day outside the compound they were trusted sons of the Almighty and true combatants; Kadu tried to make the radio work, but weak waves were detected, enough to hear typical songs sometimes interfered by voices from another radio frequency. Mardak had a difficult time trying to stop the windshield wipers, apparently the control was broke and there was no wipers either making the metal arms an incredible noise on the already scratched windshield. Upon arrival to Almanei, they knew of the four hours left to return to the compound for dinner, otherwise no food would be served until the next morning. Kadu and Hassan paired up and Mardak and Wadek were together at the fruit stand. Music was loud, and many donkeys were wondering the market. Hassan made contact with one of the venders who had a cellular phone and immediately tried to contact the Sheik back in Kastan in their native Afghanistan. The call was unsuccessful. Hassan wished to know how to get a hold of Hajak but it was just impossible. The four men knew that in order to see Hajak back again they had to stick together during the training phase and that they will be rewarded to be part of the talked plan and moved to India for instructions in how to enter the United States.

Hassan, Wadek and Mardak just walked around the market and bought many goodies while Kadu was more interested in reading the papers and magazines at one of the stands. Kadu bought a used Kalashnikov and spent almost all his money on it. They also ate good food at one of the stands. The pickup truck rolled back to the compound just on time with no problems; they were checked at the compound's checkpoint. One of the guards grabbed the recently bought Kalashnikov and made comments that it was an excellent weapon, but that was it. No problems at all. The men took their goodies to the improvised barracks and cover them with plastic since it was ready to rain. They all stopped by the dinner tent and enjoyed some fried fish. By 9pm they were in bed.

One day during the classroom training, Q'alghi announced to the combatants that the chief Alfad Dal Kaden had suffered a stroke and that he was taken to Teheran to be evaluated at the Military Hospital. The same day thousand of protestors were on the streets of Teheran protesting in front of the American Embassy against the American invasion to Iraq. Alfad Dal Kaden would never presence any other attack against the American imperialism. He was pronounced dead upon arrival to the Military Hospital. The combatants learned after the fact, that Alfad Dal Kaden was also a high ranking member of the Mujaedin organization with strong ties to governmental officials and one of the main architects of the political agenda of Kathani, the previous president of Iran. Alfad Dal Kaden was also a member of a team of researchers at the Banandali nuclear plant, one of the targets of the American and coalition forces for the past three years. Training was not suspended. They all said prayers for the chief who just joined heaven in white outfits and is joining the Almighty.

Q'alghi, proceeded with the classroom class; the topic was identifying crowd behavior in America. Late in the afternoon, a military bus entered the compound and stopped by the chief's office, this time occupied by Q'alghi. Two officers got out of the bus and approached Q'alghi indicating to him that by order of the highest clergyman, everybody in the compound should attend religious services in honor to the chief. The order was transmitted and immediately after, the combatants were getting in the bus. It departed the compound en route to Teheran.

At the American Embassy, the Assistant to the Consulate official in matters of agriculture and economics, Mr. Michael Armstrong was the first one who learned about the death of Alfad Dal Kaden. The official sent a message via fax to Washington, the same that was delivered to the CIA office where several investigations were conducted in regards to the chief's relationship with Al Q'aeda and the Al-Yamat terrorist organizations.
There was a lot of commotion on the streets and everybody seemed hurt with the chief's departure to holy places. Members of the American Embassy were watching closely the repercussion of the chief's dead in the population. Dal Kaden was not only the chief of the boot camp were terrorists are formed, but also a leader in the community, a government official, a spiritual icon, and a truly combatant for the masses of Iran. He had strong ties with Khatani, and he was trusted some of the most secretive issues in regards of the proliferation of nuclear capabilities as well as the enrichment of uranium agenda, and in matters of investigation and production of weapons of mass destruction in the region. He was a very important person in the government; he was definitely a clear target of the American government.

Back in the United States at the CIA main office in Washington, government officials started spreading the news of the death of Alfad Dal Kaden. Intelligence analysts were orienting their predictions towards a new changes or updates and following very close for the successor. Every movement done by the Iranian government was meticulously monitored and the list of candidates for the vacant position as security advisor for the Khatani regime was not vast, it just focused on one or two names as indicated by Mr. Michael Armstrong.

The crowd was not going anywhere, they were presenting their respect and admiration for the last time to Alfad Dal Kaden as the casket covered with the Iranian flag was slowly going from one point to another until it actually was placed inside a vehicle that will transport it for private religious ceremony near the president's palace in Teheran. The Kaljatahl group could not stay any longer and they were transported back to the camp to continue with their training. Tears in the eyes of the group were easily noticed and it just fed the hunger to fight even more against the imperialism and the Zionists.

The old bus was returning to the camp and the riders were singing songs of joy shouting loud the name of Alah; Kadu's sweaty face had all the signs of a rogue warrior, Hassan knew he was training for another event but this time of a bigger magnitude than the one at Lancaster University in London; after all the London event was just the testing grounds for future events; Wadek was the quiet one and his attitude and sweaty bald head can be easily confused as being afraid but his real monster was kept inside ready to pop up when hitting grounds way in the West part of the hemisphere.

It seemed like the bus took a shortcut because it made it back in less time of the predicted one; it is just a characteristic of drivers to take different routes no matter where they go just in case they are under surveillance. As a matter of fact, living in places like Iran is like walking on thin ice, it can break at any given time by your own weight or by an inflicted action. The bus parked near the man-made muddy pond and everybody was back.

As the weather changed from sunny days to dusty, windy and cold afternoons so was the mood of the instructors who came from the funeral services where they were quiet and reserved, but back at the camp they were hostiles, aggressive, and demanding. A group of combatants were tested at the obstacle course field, another group was doing drills with AK-47s and Kalashnikovs, and another group was practicing self-defense techniques. Kadu, Hassan, Wadek and Mardak were contemplating the high wooden walls they must jump as the starting point at the obstacle course area. There were rumors that a few months ago Q'alghi shot to death a trainee because he couldn't pass the wall even though he tried several times; that story was preoccupying Hassan who was a little overweight. But, there was no problem at all at the end, these true warriors that came all the way from Afghanistan were essential elements picked by Sheik Lazur almad Al Fanistar; their spirit was high, their motivation was outstanding, their objectives were clear, their decision in doing the things right was already pre-tested, their exposure to danger was not something to worry about, and their loyalty was stamped in their minds and hearts.

They were killing machines, they could operate individually as a one man-team, and they were masters of techniques such as survival, evasion, resistance, and escape. Part of the training was upgraded to a more sophisticated way to infiltrate and to escape from the enemy lines damaging the central nervous system of the military apparatus. The main square or formation area had three flag poles, the Iranian flag in the highest pole; the camp flag on the right side of the highest pole, and the American flag half-way up, symbolizing the numerous lost of human lives and that on every Friday afternoon before the training was over, the flag was brought down and burned by the trainees.

It symbolizes the end of another successful week for the trainees, celebrating with songs against democracy and against the imperialism and capitalism.

In a village nearby, members of the Hamas terrorist organization were watching television in one of the jewelry stores, and find out that the United States government expressed their comfort after learning that Alfad Dal Kaden was dead and that the American intelligence community had the opportunity to easily interdict the Iranian government to monitor all activities and affairs from the space. Hamas members were rushing to the camp and met with Q'alghi, this time to talk face to face with the man that once before emptied out his magazines while training them to let him know about the American perception. For some reason, Hamas members as well as other members of different terrorist organizations had contact with Q'alghi when news were important either for advice or for common evaluation and follow up of events as part of their intelligence strategy.

The trainees were experiencing their last two weeks at the camp and getting the flavor of the fabrication of explosives, a very intensive course of ten hours per day for five days, which includes classroom training and field training under the supervision of an elite team from the Iranian Army. The regime of Khatani was a persistent support for the preparation of terrorists to be utilized against the Western hemisphere; members of the Hamas, Abu Nidal and Al-Yamat terrorist organizations have trained in the Iranian isolated fields.
Q'alghi was evaluating the alternative of sending the Kaljatahl group back to Afghanistan prior to their trip to India in order to assassinate Mr. Karl Blastorm, the American senior advisor for security operations.

The plan for the four Afghan warriors was to leave Iran with fake passports, survey the movements of the American official everywhere he goes and ambush his motorcade, and to leave Afghanistan en route to India with different passports for which the help of the Sheik was needed due to his wise influence and contacts with the Iranian government.

The four Afghan warriors knew than in a few days they will be reunited again with Hajak somewhere in Florida in the United States of America for the initiation of Phase Two of the plan. As well as them, Hajak prepared his part during all these absent days from Afghanistan and while the four combatants of the Kaljatahl group were training in Iran. He will be added to the group as the fifth member and leader of the operations for the second phase of the terrorist plan.

Sheik Lazur almad Al-Fanistar reunited members of his organization for spiritual support to the initiation of Phase Two and for the almost successful culmination of Phase One in Iran and in Tampa, Florida. Both preparations for the operation took place at the same time. The next chapter explains how well business went in Florida.

Near the city of Kastan, back in Afghanistan, the Sheik was mesmerized with all the reports sent by Hajak from Tampa, but it didn't surprise him that the United States of America still not prepared to fight terrorism adequately and efficiently. Even though the results of September 11, 2001 were devastating and the creation of the new homeland security entity with billions of dollars allocated for the fight against terrorism and for the protection of the American citizens, still are enormous gaps in the security system of the ports, in this case, and that sufficient training wasn't even necessary to attack one more time our national interests. The flavor of victory was even closer to the leaders and spiritual advisors of Al-Yamat and Al Q'aeda.

The entire operation started to shape better everyday; as it was masterminded by the Sheik, four men trained in Iran, one man trained and infiltrated in Tampa, all five men will meet in Florida, they will meet to analyze the situation and prior to carry on with the plan, a sixth man will appear as the only representative of the Sheik to make sure the operation was carry out as ordered.

It seemed that the reports sent to the Sheik by Hajak from Tampa, made his faith even more confident than ever before. This information was transmitted to Q'alghi, who immediately informed the men of the Kaljatahl group to enhance their confidence. One night during training, the four men were exposed to amphibious operations to include basics of diving, light search and rescue, under berth explosives, and swimming with equipment and Kadu expressed his concerns about a recon prior to carry on with the plan; Q'alghi informed him that when in Florida, there will be enough time to recon the entire port as if it was their own homes; the only thing that was not set yet was the date and time of the attack, which will be the sole responsibility and decision of the sixth man, the Sheik's representative.

Upon culmination of the training, the Kaljatahl group was transferred to the province of Khorasan, north east of Iran to rest for a couple of days at an exclusive spa and to devote all the remaining time in Iran to prayers, mental relaxation and last preparation before departure to India. Q'alghi was with them and his naughty attitude and rebel appearance was left at the camp; this time he was friendly, extremely supportive and attentive to all the concerns the combatants had.

The first day they had and early light breakfast by the pool-side couches follow by a half day in the spa. At the steam bath, Wadek reaffirmed his confidence with the rest stating that he has never felt so full of love for the Muslim cause and that he was ready to do everything he could to eliminate all enemies of Islam even if he has to sacrifice his own life. There were no silent moments and everybody reaffirmed their confidence by shouting the name of Allah. They were a timing bomb at once, the one that was always underestimated by the government of United States of America.

In the afternoon and after the sunset, the men visited Mashhad, the capital of Khorasan, bought some fresh fruit at the local market and some books for the long journey. They didn't know at that point the disjunctive of returning to Afghanistan and eliminate the American official Michael Armstrong or if they had to travel directly to India. Only the Sheik could know that and order any movements. On the second night, Q'alghi advised the four combatants that the Sheik put a halt to their return to Afghanistan for undisclosed reasons and that their departure to India the next morning was imminent. It was time to pack. Q'alghi provided the men with their passports, their names where the same and maybe one or two letters were omitted or added to slightly change their true identity.

The next morning they departed Mashhad and went directly to the airport in two vehicles, Kadu and Hassan with a local taxi, and Wadek and Mardak with Q'alghi aboard a rented vehicle. When airport loud speakerphones announced the boarding time, Q'alghi kissed and hugged the four men and at this time he was not sure if he will ever see the Kaljatahl group again.

Wadek was the first man in line and walked to the plane with firm steps followed by Kadu, Mardak and then Hassan, who thanked Q'alghi one more time for the tough training and for the encouragement he injected in the combatants' mind everyday during their stay at the camp; he just turned around at the door before the gangway and told Q'alghi: "We will be back soon".

About twenty-five minutes later, the Iran Aseman flight number 2211 was already in the air en route to Calcutta International Airport. Wadek was sitting in row 25 having by his side an old lady dressed in some type of religious outfit, Hassan and Mardak in row 27, and Kadu in row 32 almost at the back of the plane by the window. The man sitting next to Kadu was reading the Islamic Post, usually printed in the United States who in a calm, but firm voice told Kadu: "I was told that the Kaljatahl group was the best". Kadu, who had his head leaning against the window almost jumped from his seat, while the unknown man told him to relax. He then continued and informed Kadu that the Sheik was very proud of them and gave him an envelope containing $5,000 dollars. He told Kadu, that the man responsible to transport them from the Calcutta Airport to the hotel was Mahattar Sharkahan, a.k.a. "Sharka" and that they should not make contact with anybody else.

Very few words were said while flying, since the unknown man was with his eyes closed and his head leaning against the comfortable pillow. Kadu tried to make eye contact with the rest of the group but he was unsuccessful. A brief conversation was taken place in row 27, and Hassan was imagining the feelings and courage Ali Ata may had experienced when flying the American Airlines jet in the low skies of New York. Mardak affirmed: "America allowed us to have martyrs, heroes, and eternal spirits for the Almighty".

Sharka was already at the Calcutta International Airport, about two hours earlier. He visited some airport stores and constantly checked his watch; he was not feeling comfortable in doing what he was about to do, transporting terrorists from the airport to a hotel. But, Sharka was previously advised by the members of the Al-Yamat terrorist organization that he needed to prove himself by doing small details as such in order to be part of them. He checked his watch again. Suddenly, and after many walks from right to left in the dirty hallways of the terminal, Sharka heard the announcing of the arrival of flight # 2211 and immediately ceased all movements.

He approached the gate where the flight was supposed to arrive and sat in the lobby area. The unknown man in the plane told Kadu that all four men should walk slowly while in the first lobby as soon as leaving the plane and to walk towards the phone booth on the right hand side, where Sharka was sitting and carrying a black leather bag with the shoulder strap across his chest. The contact was clear and without any danger. Sharka welcomed the Kaljatahl group and directed them to the parking lot. No words were exchanged; the four combatants just followed Sharka to the green Land Rover. Things turned different when in the vehicle; they were laughing, talking and sharing information regarding their new temporary home in India. The vehicle took Labantan Avenue and stopped at the intersection of Shirti Street where the four stars hotel Salman Yatar awaited the combatants. They all were checked in Suite 920 located on the last floor. A round cherry table with lots of fruit was the décor of what was about to become, the table of negotiations for the next seven days.

Sharka sat at the end of the table overlooking Shirti Street and without wasting time began the conversation. He advised the four combatants to enjoy their free time limited to the installation of the hotel, instead of going outside; the closer they get to the operation the more careful they had to be. Sharka explained that a Greek company hired the services of a Panamanian vessel to transport 50,000 tons of dry cement from Greece to the United States via the port of Tampa in Florida and that the crew members were from India and Pakistan, as their new passports showed a different nationality. They were to be picked up in two to three days to start their journey to Greece.

Sheik Lazur almad Al Fanistar sent some instructions to the combatants with the unknown man in the plane that seated besides Kadu. But, as per the Sheik, those instructions were to be given only after they were at the hotel and that if no inconvenience arose. The unknown man knew everything, and he just went to the room and knocked. Sharka opened and let him in. The unknown man pulled out an envelope from his dark jacket and gave it to Sharka. This man proceeded with the meeting and informed to them what the Sheik wanted them to know. The plan was to travel to the United States with the vessel posting as crew members and to make contact with Hajak in Tampa. They were enthusiastic and little concern that something would go wrong; their level of confidence was high and their prayers never stopped. By the end of the week, Sharka gather the information that the Xanadu, the vessel, was the one assigned for the transportation of the dry cement to a company by the name of American Python, one of the tenant companies in the port of Tampa.

The day of the departure of the Kaljatahl group was Saturday morning, and there were no problems encountered, everything went right. An hour later, the prayers were heard from India to the little town of Kastan in Afghanistan, a place where the Sheik was also praying for the men and the cause.

The journey was about to begin. The Xanadu was already docked in the Indian port from a previous trip to the region. The Kaljatahl group was to be trained aboard in the different areas regarding the normal business; they had one month to learn everything before the vessel arrived to the United States.

The journey to Greece was somehow scary, the weather was bad and it seemed that the trip was to be postponed; but, they never asked questions, they had to go with the flow. The Captain was not aware, neither the entire crew of the precedence of the terrorist group already aboard. Somehow they manage to dock at the Greek port of Zorba and business was going as usual. Berth 250 was getting busy and the tenant, Python Group, was ready to start the preparation to pump the dry material from its silos into the vessel compartments. Python Group has been in the business of cement production for over 100 years in Europe, and one of the major producers of the material in Greece. Their sister-company was in the United States under the name of American Python, also a producer of these material plus many other aggregate materials throughout over forty different plants along the east coast of the United States.

It took six days to pump in the dry cement into the vessel. While in Greece, the members of the Kaljatahl group enjoyed some good time at a nearby brothel and bar and always sealing their commitment to a great cause by cheering loud Islamic thoughts. They were free to go from the vessel to the surrounding areas of the port, and they had orders that if anything went wrong the only person they should contact was Sharka, who had an undisclosed alternate plan for the safety of the group and the operation. They just had to be more careful who to deal with when having fun. The night before the departure, the members of the group slept at a local motel after a night of sex, alcohol, dance, and meditation.

Early in the morning of a Saturday day, they were aboard the vessel, and Sharka said goodbye to them and wished them luck. The three weeks journey to the United States of America was imminent and a reality.

TAMPA, FLORIDA, U.S.A.
"Testing the Waters"

During the past couple of months of his separation from the Kaljatahl group while in Iran, Hajak, the ex-Captain in the new reformed Afghan police force and who used to work together with the coalition forces led by Major Hegedus was dedicating his time to follow step by step the meticulous plan the Sheik had for him in order to have part of the second phase of the plan prepared prior to the arrival of the Kaljatahl group to the port of Tampa.

Hajak was very familiar with the entire city and the surroundings due to a previous residence with his father while the old man was attending local universities and medical conferences in the past.

Hajak had three weeks left to continue what he was doing prior to be the host of his long-time brothers traveling aboard the Xanadu vessel.

Hajak was attending the University of Tampa taking some courses in oceanography, nothing of his interest really, but because the contact he had with professor Abdul Sahkir, a fifteen years veteran with the educational entity and originally from a small Palestinian settlement near the town of Tyre in Lebanon.

Abdul Sahkir served as part of a United Nations multinational force in Lebanon during the decade of the 70's as a result of the intervention of it to cease the fight between Lebanon and the occupied forces of Israel. The professor was responsible of the translation and interpretation of Palestinian documents into French, and English that subsequently ended up on the desk of one of the top commanders of the allied forces in Beirut.

He enjoyed most of his free time partying with French servicemen, and some troops from the Senegal and Ghana detachment. His Muslim origins and spiritual faith was as strong as the rockets traveling from Israel to downtown Beirut.

Later on, during the early eighties he met an American lady by the name of Stella Malinowski, who was of polish descendants and a very articulated and educated woman serving with the American detachment to the United States in Beirut. They got married and she was his passport to America, a long-time desire of him to know and to see at first hand what in the Middle East is considered the roots of sin, the threat to Islam and the cradle of evil that is a threat to the entire Muslim population in the world. Sahkir and Stella finished their tour in Beirut and settled for several months in the beautiful beaches of Marbella in Spain. They both were working for a non-too active office of the United Nations in Spain. It was just a transition and a relaxing moment in their lives prior to move to the United States where Stella actually wanted to live. She never knew, even though she possessed great intelligence and counter-intelligence and espionage background about the intimate and spiritual desires of Sahkir to know more about the United States and to feel the hatred at first hand.

He was also a great friend and spiritual follower of Sheik Lazud almar Al-Fanistar organization in Beirut during his teen years and early twenties and never lost contact with some of the followers. He knew from early years, that sooner or later Allah would provide him with an opportunity to be a soldier of the Muslim world and that his courage and commitment would be needed for the sake of his brothers and the future of Islam. Now he knew, that the opportunity was coming even faster, and that his transfer to the United States was imminent. He decided to contact his brothers in Beirut.

In a French coffee place on Hamrah Street in Beirut called Café La Paix, a middle age man by the name of Salmad received a phone call from Abdul Sahkir who prompted him about his whereabouts and desires to participate in the fight against the imperialism since he was ready to travel to the United States with an American wife. Salmad, a long-time friend and brother of Abdul never doubted about his courage and decided to notify the Sheik back in Afghanistan.

Several months passed and no indication from the Sheik was received and Abdul departed the Spanish territory en route to the city of Tampa in Florida. Stella parents lived in the city of Brandon located on the east side of the city of Tampa and they settled near her parents' house and were ready to initiate their new lives. This is how Abdul got into the United States and now it was a matter of time before he gets an orientation in how to participate in the fight against the imperialism. His situation was something that could not be underestimated by the Sheik since Abdul was a satellite already in the heart of the enemy nation and can not be forgotten, but to be considered as another key element for their eternal commitment.

His teaching background and degrees earned in Europe and in the Middle East got him a job as an assistant at the University of Tampa, where he was welcomed by the minority of Muslims. Later on, the connection between Hajak and the professor became more than the regular educator to student; they were spiritual fighters for the same cause.

Abdul Sahkir had to learn how to live with an occult lifestyle totally different from the one shared with Stella. She got into a family business and was working at a hotel in Brandon.

As a surprise for Abdul, he received the long-waiting call from Salmad who mentioned to him that his conversation with the Sheik was successful but with limitations to the plan since the true warriors were already trained and that his participation instead, would be of hosting them, open a bank account and made all the arrangements necessary that for one reason or another it was miscalculated or omitted within the plan.

That was enough for him. No Muslim looked that their level of participation in a plan is more important than other members, they all have different jobs but they know that the commitment and efficiency of every step of the plan no matter what it is, it is important and that the key element for the success as a whole is unity.

That was the time when Hajak was ordered to make contact with the professor. This was the time when the professor learned that a team of four warriors were aboard the Xanadu, and that a couple weeks later they would be arriving at the port of Tampa. Hajak updated the magistrate with the details of the mission. The Sheik had already revealed the mission: the complete destruction of the Port of Tampa.

The Port of Tampa is by far the largest port in the State of Florida when measured by cargo tonnage throughput, handling over 50 million tons of cargo per year. This equals approximately 50% of all cargo that moves through Florida ports. The terrorists' mission was targeted to something big, capable to paralyze the economy immediately, to discredit the efficiency of the Department of Homeland Security, to deliver a low punch to the White House, and to demonstrate to the outside world that business means business.

Hajak was living in an efficiency right out of route 60 just a few hundred yards from I-75 and he used to frequent the famous Barnes & Noble bookstore located nearby to enjoy fresh literature, especially about the Floridian region where he was staying, about American politics, and reading books about terrorism. During his stay in Tampa, he knew exactly which restaurants and fast food restaurants did not have surveillance cameras, being these places the most appropriate for short eating sessions or to meet anybody at anytime. He used to take several rides along the city to observe police patrols during the day, during the afternoon and during the graveyard hours. It didn't take too long to notice that several police vehicles got the parking lot of the local Dunkin Donuts occupied, as well as the ones in the nearby coffee shop in Ybor City. He was once stopped by a female police, a chubby blond lady with nasty attitude, who got the front seat of her patrol vehicle full of fat-cakes and soda cans, because he didn't stop completely at a stop sign. He knew he couldn't argue and signed the ticket, the same that was paid the very next morning. A few weeks later he observed that the fat cop was entering his favorite store for books, and she was sitting on a couch reading a mystery book but falling asleep at the same time. Hajak, got three books related to how to lose weight, and healthy cooking and placed them in the coffee desk at her right side and under her purse. He then left.

When Hajak made contact with the professor, this one informed him that the bank account was already opened at a local bank under Sahkir's name, same bank where this one and Stella had a joined account. Money was coming from Iran and from Afghanistan directly to the account and Hajak got free access thanks to an ATM card giving to him by the professor.

They usually met at the university's cafeteria for very brief chats, generally to establish the time and place where they would be meeting the same night for dinner. One Tuesday night, they were having some pizza at a local place with no surveillance cameras and Hajak was informing him about the entire plan. He told the professor a little bit of Wadek, Mardak, Kadu and Hassan, the Kaljatahl group as named by the Sheik. They both agreed that the mission to destroy the port of Tampa might take longer time than the one predicted. Also, they knew that no operation would take place until the spiritual leader and head of the operation in the name of the Sheik arrives to Tampa, somebody they didn't know who he was. In the meantime, Hajak continued with his mission and part of the operative. He already gathered the necessary information such as maps from the port, the name of every tenant in the port, the name of the security company working at the gates, the roughly amount of officers from port authority, and the small team of sheriff deputies going in and out.

Hajak was gathering information on each particular tenant putting more emphasis in American Python, the recipient of the dry cement coming from Greece aboard the Xanadu vessel, where the Kaljatahl group was aboard. All four members of the group had visas and they knew they could meet with Hajak as soon as the vessel arrives.

The professor was also a member of the Muslim mosque in a nearby rural town and invited Hajak for prayers and more plans. Hajak enjoyed most of the reunions. This was a place to charge their spirits and motivation by shouting anti-American themes that were always the basics of the reunion, legally permitted and protected by the first amendment and by the constitution of a nation that was suffering the consequences of terrorism. There was no better place for the discharge of hatred against America and the Zionists, than in the same American soil and ironically, to be protected. This was a reality. This still is a reality.

It was less than a week of waiting for the Xanadu to arrive. Hajak and the professor met at the Mosque one more time; this time, they were meeting with an individual by the name of Abad who was bringing fake identification cards for the members of the Kaljatahl group and a driver's license for Hajak. All photos were previously sent by the Sheik and this is how the identification cards were made, and they were real numbers assigned.

Abad came all the way from Miami where he and a couple cousins run a shady business.

At the Mosque, a very low profile was kept by all official members, and the general public attended the place for their religious service without bothering anybody. The previous night of the arrival, Hajak could not sleep well, something was bothering him, as he was watching CNN he learned that the homeland security alertness level was raised due to some intelligence reports that revealed possible attacks to the mass transit in the United States. But, as usual, this only was taken into big consideration in cities like New York City, New Jersey, Washington, Los Angeles, Denver, Atlanta, Houston, and Chicago. Tampa was not mentioned, it was not the place where terrorists actually live or work, at least this is how certain minor cities are considered, but appreciated by terrorist organizations.

Hajak rented a white van and placed on it a magnet sign that showed a fictitious company name. It read: Atlantic Environmental Services, Inc. and a phone number, which was actually Hajak's pre-paid cellular phone that he bought at K-Mart since his arrival to Tampa. His level of confidence was amazing and it showed no fear, he was a really professional, a mercenary, a terrorist. A cool Saturday morning in November 2004, Hajak made a phone call to professor Sahkir to inform him that he was going to Ybor City to have breakfast and to wait there for the arrival of the Kaljatahl group. The professor, after talking to him, called the Sheik to tell him that the plan was going in the right direction and about the assigned tasks to each and every single cell member. Tampa was about to host one of the bloodiest and dangerous terrorist organizations in the world.

The Kaljatahl group had the same training and philosophy that Al Q'aeda, Al-Yamat, Mujaedhin, and similar Middle Eastern organizations that tremendously oppose to democracy and freedom as form of government and that are committed to the destruction of the United States as well as Israel for the abuses, as they considered, were committed against the Muslim world and the region after the introduction of troops in Iraq. The war was a clear an imminent event. About two-o'clock in the afternoon, the Xanadu was awaiting for clearance from the Coast Guard to dock at Berth-519, the one assigned to American Python.

As part of usual business, two members of the port authority force were at the berth, one van with two members from US Customs, and a pick-up truck with two in-house security officers from the company receiving the material. It was amazing to notice that the people we expect to see more attentive were the ones that seemed less professionals and interested in the events. Just by looking at their composure and concentration, the two security officers were the most attentive and concentrated to their assignment. They were trained officers in Maritime Security (MARSEC) on behalf of their assets at the port of Tampa. The two officers, Corporate Security Specialist Rudy Milano and Corporate Security Specialist George Nestor were the ones assigned to the protection of the berth, monitoring of the crew including both the ones with visas that were allowed to leave the embarkation and the detainees, as referred to the ones without visas.

At 2:30 pm, the vessel was officially docked and a group of line-handlers were stabilizing the embarkation. US Customs went inside the ship and started their normal routine of inspecting it, to check for the authorized crew in accordance to their manifest, searching for the possibility of drugs, explosives, or illegal aliens. A bomb-detection K-9 was accompanying the officers and the search began.

A few people from the 30 crew members were seen at the bridge and some of them close to the gangway area of the ship, none of them were from the Kaljatahl group. The afternoon was kind of sunny and humid, and about three employees from American Python were also at the berth ready to initiate their security duties right after US Customs personnel finish clearing the ship. It was a normal business day for everybody. It was the type of day with the characteristics desired by the enemy forces to infiltrate terrorists.

After thirty-five minutes, US Custom officers abandoned the ship and handled one copy of the manifest to Mr. Carlos Gappa, the agent of American Python, and one copy for the security officers. That was the end of the responsibilities for the experts in homeland security. The Custom officers got into the van and departed en route to their detachment at the other side of the port. Everything was ready to initiate operations to start pumping out the 50,000 tons of dry cement into the silos, a task of about seven days long counting with good weather conditions and free of equipment malfunctioning. This was the beginning of the one week time frame for the terrorists aboard the vessel to make contact and the necessary arrangements for the big plan to come later on. The captain of the ship, Altaraban Ghandaran, originally from Pakistan was the man in charge of twenty-nine more men, five from Pakistan, eleven from China, six from India, three from Ukraine, and the four combatants from Afghanistan.

The regular business started when the employees from American Python started to hook up the hoses and to run the compressors for the initiation of the pumping. Security Specialist Rudy Milano stayed on duty for the next twelve hours while George Nestor went back to the hotel to rest; his shift was scheduled to start at 3 am.

In the meantime, Hajak finished the last cup of coffee and walked to the van parked two blocks south on 7th Avenue in Ybor City and drove towards the port on 21st Street. At the main entrance, an old gentleman, in his mid-60's, tired of being on his feet, sweaty and thirsty and with no much enthusiasm about working, was the so-called security officer in-charge of the access control at the port. The actual port authority officer was not nearby, leaving all entrance lanes at the mercy of the security officers working for a private security company.

It is amazing and incredible to know and to accept that in a nation that has been hit so hard with terrorism, there is no much emphasis and attention to the main point of access to such an important and sensitive place. Hajak knew that, and all he had to say was that he was going to Berth-519 to the Xanadu vessel that requested the services of Atlantic Environmental Services, Inc. The old man re-directed him to the port authority building to get a pass. Hajak went to the building located a few feet away from the main entrance, got in the building where another old-man was in charge of the picture taking and from the same security company as the ones at the gates. There was no verification of services needed from the port authority office with any of the tenants-company inside the port. Hajak was photographed and issued a pass with an illegible photo and drove to the gates. He was in.

After entering, he knew that nobody was going to pay attention to him at all. After driving less than quarter of a mile inside the port and in a deserted area, he suddenly stopped the van, got out of it and removed the only magnetic sign that read Atlantic Environmental Services, Inc. before proceeding to Berth-519. Upon his arrival to the berth, Security Specialist Milano stopped the van to process Hajak according to company policies.

This was an opportunity for Hajak to learn about the procedures and the way all visitors were processed when already inside the port. He noticed a big difference between the American Python Security Specialist and the security guards from the private company responsible of the access control at the port main entrance. Milano's attentiveness and alertness levels were too high, but necessary. Hajak informed him that he was there to pick-up four crew members, all of them with visas. Already aware of the white van, Kadu, who was having a cigarette nearby the first aid station close to the gangway alerted the other members and proceeded to descend from the vessel.

Milano logged them all after verifying that all of them were legally admitted to the United States. The white van did not have any company sign visible anymore; he was just an ordinary man picking up ordinary visitors. Already at the berth, Kadu, Hassan, Wadek, and Mardak were processed by Milano. The Kaljatahl group has legally arrived to the USA.

There wasn't too much enthusiasm at the beginning, but while in the van the members of the terrorist group were given hugs and kisses to the driver as they were happy to see him again after so long. Hajak drove the combatants to a motel in the city of Brandon, fifteen minutes to the East from the port. At the motel's parking lot, Hajak informed the men to watch their composure and to listen to the man they are about to meet inside Room-320. All five men got in the elevator taking them up to the third and last floor. Hajak knocked before opening the door and waited until the professor, Abdul Sahkir gave him the okay to enter the room. While inside the room, all six men cheered and elevated prayers to the Almighty, the Creator, and the Merciful.

The four terrorists that just arrived learned about their respective roles while in the port and that for order of the Sheik, they were to return to India with the ship upon finishing the delivery of the dry cement to the American company. The Sheik wanted to test the waters first, evaluate the system pertaining to immigration, port authority state of alertness and shift work quantity members, routes of escape from the primary target location, the process and requirements necessary to open bank accounts, public and private transportation, all points of access to the port, location of the most vulnerable points, accessibility to sensitive areas, and everything else to complete the entire project. The group learned that they will be back to the same port by the end of the following month delivering the same kind of material to the same company using the same berth and probably facing the same security officers.

So, time was running out and the professor disclosed the roles to be accomplished to perfection. After a smooth zip of vodka on the rocks, Sahkir started to talk by stating: Kadu, you will be in charge to record the number of security officials to include private security, in-house security, port authority, sheriff vehicles, customs rounds, coast guard rounds, etc., and to establish a pattern in their routine for ten days. All the information will be recorded in his personal laptop. The professor had another zip of vodka and continued: Hassan, you will be in charge of the photo and video surveillance utilizing always the American Python silos as the main landmark and starting point to shoot quadrants that will include the entire area where the combustible is stored. He then continued without drinking, Wadek and Mardak will work as a team by using the installations at the port such as the seaman's club, the port ministries shuttle, and touring the areas where combustible is stored, and the areas where chemicals are loaded into tankers ready to roll on the railroad tracks.

These tasks were to be performed from the time they got up in the morning until the time they go back to bed. All six men left the motel en route to eat Japanese food in the town of Lithia. At the table, imported beer was their choice followed by steak, sushi, and fish. Also, the professor wanted to know from any of the group members if they knew the mysterious man already assigned by the Sheik several months ago to be the leader of the operations. They all were aware that a leader was to be present anytime soon to coordinate the entire plan as a result of the intelligence collection and analysis of the plan in Afghanistan. They mentioned several possible names, but nobody knew that the man assigned was somebody coming back from the death: Alfad Dal Kaden, the Chief of the boot camp in Iran where the Kaljatahl group trained. The US Department of State added this name to the long list of terrorists already captured or dead as a result of the questionable long war against international terrorism. Alfad was hiding in the rocky-mountains north of Kabul and had met Osama bin Laden in two opportunities to have his blessings for the upcoming event.

The terrorist organization is extremely attentive to leaks and their intelligence apparatus is based on patriotism and spiritual strength, something way too far from American counterpart due to their inexperience in counterterrorism operations. Alfad Dal Kaden was ready to fly from Teheran to London, from London to Montreal, and from Montreal to Newark.

After dinner, Hajak advised the professor to return to the hotel while he takes the four men back to the port. All four men were transported back to the port. At the main entrance, the van entered without a pass, and the old security guard didn't recognized the driver from his previous entry as a member of the Atlantic Environmental Services Company.

This time, he just said that he was driving back a four men crew to the Xanadu docked in Berth-519. The guard looked inside the van, checked their passports and allowed them entry. Twelve feet away from the gate, an armed port authority officer ignored completely the event that just happened; he was talking on his cell phone facing the other way.

American Python Security Specialist Rudy Milano stopped the van and immediately recognized the men and welcomed them back with a smile. Wadek gave him a plastic bag containing a six-pack of coke and a bag of chips; Rudy accepted and saw the men going up the gangway, while the van was already departing.

Captain Altaraban Ghandaran's involvement was very clear; he assigned the four combatants as a support unit while the rest of the crew had different jobs to do. For the next eight to ten days, Kadu was to spend time at the bridge to record the daily patrols, frequency of checks by port authority, lunch time and activities during this break time by members of the company's security department, and all security activities by any agency. Hassan had to climb to the very top of the crane and stay at the operator's cabin filming and photographing the area where the combustible tanks were located without security.

The next morning, everybody started with their respective assignments. Hassan promptly noticed a small airport located northwest of his position where helicopters and small planes took off and landed constantly. Wadek and Mardak were waiting for the port ministries shuttle van for a short tour of the port. Kadu was very busy logging in the frequency of port authority checks to the area. Rudy Milano was already sleeping at the hotel. This time, the Security Specialist on duty was George Nestor, who was outside the vehicle walking and observing the small embarkations traffic near the berth. Kadu noticed that this officer is the only one who spend time outside the patrol vehicle in many opportunities compared to Rudy Milano who spent the twelve hours shift inside the vehicle. All four men were going out for dinner with Hajak around 8 pm.

Hajak approached the gate at the port and this time he was greeted by a port authority officer, who asked him for his driver's license in order to allow him entry. While recording the driver's license on a clipboard, Hajak was telling him that he was going to pick up four crew members from the Xanadu vessel. The officer returned the document to Hajak and allowed him access without pronouncing a word. The port authority officer never checked for the vessel name in his master list, never checked the van even though the MARSEC level (Maritime Security) was only of Level-I and it requires random checks, therefore Hajak was already in. From the gate until the time he approached Berth-519, he was imagining that the van was loaded with explosives. He knew it was an easy thing to do.

Security Specialist George Nestor stopped the van an ordered the driver out of the vehicle. Hajak was surprised, but complied without any objections. The officer inspected the van quickly and noticed nothing wrong with it. He just didn't like the Middle Eastern accent and appearance of the driver, but covered his instincts with his normal duties and security responsibilities. The Kaljatahl group was ready to leave and they were processed in order by Officer Nestor. This officer noticed that the only person taking something with him was Kadu, who carried a manila folder containing some papers. The men entered the van and made some comments about the attentiveness of Officer Nestor as they were leaving the area.

Professor Sahkir was already sitting at the dinner table at a local diner near the bookstore, where he previously purchased some tour guides from the Tampa area and was very interested in flight tours, something that was also suggested by the Sheik. The men were hungry; promptly, the table was served with fish and exotic seafood dishes, chicken, corn bread, rice and beans, and beers. The first reports were given to professor Sahkir and the white pages were not white anymore; barbecue sauce and portions of Sahkir's fingerprints were latent.

Hassan made the comment of the nearby airport were small planes and helicopters landed constantly. The professor advised them that the Sheik was not too eager to conduct air attack since this is an area where the Americans were emphasizing a lot in security. As the Sheik used to say: "…When your adversary covers his face with both hands, you have only one second to hit him either in the stomach or destroy his ribs on the side". Hassan brought up the issue because he though stealing a plane to flight it for less than a mile would never give time to the federal agencies to react on time. The only issue was who would be the one called for self-immolation. At this time, Wadek never doubted and volunteered if that was the case. The only explosive to be used was the entire fuel of the plane against the combustible or chemical reservoirs.
The Sheik called the professor and advised to continue with the same plan and routine, and requested all the possible information acquired by the Kaljatahl group. All the collection of information was sent via fax from the professor's own residence to the Sheik's office, and then the documents were analyzed by him, Alfad Dal Kaden, and several spiritual and military leaders.
Mardak and Wadek, explained that their first tour to the port was like going to Disney, no security at all in any of the tenants installations, with the exception of a company that deals with

foreign vehicles that have one armed guard at its main entrance. They noticed a preferred point of reunion for the sheriff's vehicle, where an old officer always has his newspapers wide open reading it inside the cruiser. That reunion point was identified in a map, and coordinates were traced from the silos to it, including the time to reach each point at several speed limits.

Dinner was excellent, and a second round of fresh chicken in a basket was at the table, with it a second round of imported beers for all the combatants.

Officer George Nestor, at the port, grabbed a yogurt and swallowed it in five seconds. He grabbed another one from the cooler on the back seat of his patrol vehicle along with a sandwich bag containing several pieces of Italian salami, cappiccola, pepperoncini, prosciuto, goat cheese and Edam cheese. That was his dinner.

The van approached the main entrance to the port. A young Haitian security officer with tennis shoes and in uniform was also wearing a black jacket normally for cold weather areas. He seemed bored and also hungry, Hajak told him that he was dropping four crew members from the Xanadu vessel and immediately offered the guard a container with smelly chicken leftovers that he accepted it with a smile. The guard rested the clipboard on top of the food container and logged the driver's information; they were in. Officer George Nestor stopped the van, observed the men descending it and ordered the van to leave the area while he was to process the returning crew.

He asked Kadu: "Where is your manila folder?", Kadu responded with a little surprise: "I threw it away, it was nothing important". The men were allowed to board the Xanadu.

The rest of the days went by collecting information and delivering it to the Sheik. The scope of the entire business at the port was an easy task to perform; entrances, roads, railroad tracks, stop signs, empty lots, open areas, green areas, police stations, berths location, hidden places, and other icons were necessary for the formulation of an infallible attack plan.

Back in Afghanistan, the Sheik ordered Alfad Dal Kaden, who had a different appearance, with no mustache and no beard, wearing jeans and shirts, carrying a CD player on his belt and a cellular phone, to start preparing his stuff to depart promptly from Teheran; he was supposed to meet with Hajak and Sahkir in Tampa in less than twenty days. By then, the Kaljatahl group was to be half-way back to India were they would remain for another training with Al Q'aeda.

Hajak and the professor were at the University of Tampa spending time in classes and the bookstore getting away from the plan for a small period of time and getting involved with their curricula at the institution. The day of the departure was close. The night before the six men reunited again for dinner at a famous Italian restaurant in downtown Tampa.
All men were aware of their return to India to train while the plan was still cooking in Afghanistan and while the Chief of the operation was en route to Tampa in the next twenty days.
Lots of garlic bread was ordered, chicken parmesan, seafood linguini, fried calamari a-la putanesca, ravioli with meat sauce and eggplant al-forno, with three bottles of Pinot Grillo; there was no doubt that the combatants knew how to fill their bellies at all times.

The men arrived back to the port around midnight. They were rapidly processed at the main entrance, but they were strictly processed and observed by Officer Nestor, who ordered the van to leave immediately. He processed one by one and thanked them for their cooperation and wished them good luck and a safe return to wherever they go.

The Kaljatahl group had accomplished their mission of testing the waters for the upcoming plan. Early in the morning, the vessel was inspected by Custom officials and released from the port an hour later. The Xanadu was en route to India. Officer Nestor went back to the hotel. The professor and Hajak were back to the University. The Sheik had everything he needed and Alfad Dal Kaden was already flying from Teheran.

AFGHANISTAN
"Regrouping"

The American troops were attacking the red zone of Szekistan after intelligence reports indicated that in that particular area there was a stockpile of Kalashnikovs and AK-47's along with mines, bazookas and grenade launchers ready to be transported to Kabul and to be used by the Taliban against the coalition forces. The British army deployed one platoon of infantrymen, the Australian army had already one platoon of special-forces men and the United States Army deployed one platoon of rangers. A total of 90 elements went to Szekistan under the command of Major Hegedus, a long time friend of Hajak when in the police force in Afghanistan.

Major Hegedus seized all the weapons and arrested thirty-five males and four females after defeating a strong resistance that left over sixty civilians and eleven military dead. His report, that was later released from the camp-press to the outside world detailed two military men dead and over one hundred terrorists dead. The prisoners were taken for interrogation to the Mozak prison camp, the military center Major Hegedus was in charge. The females were placed in individual cells in Block-Alpha, while the men in one cell located in Block-Sigma. In between areas the main building was the operations center for Major Hegedus to direct all operations in the fifth quadrant of the region.

One Friday night, after having the prisoners locked up without interrogation and without provided them with food and water for three days, Sergeant Glen Rostov ordered one of the females out of the cell and took her to the main building were she was ordered to shower in plain view of the military men. She was hosed down with cold water and Rostov put some shampoo on her long hair.

Her nipples were hard and covered with the bubbles from the shampoo. Rostov handled her a towel; then he hugged the woman, feeling her wet breasts over his sweaty camouflage shirt. The woman didn't say a word; she couldn't anyway; Rostov stuck his tongue in her mouth and kissed her like if he was in love with her for many years. Then, he abruptly slapped the woman in the face and threw her on the wet floor of the improvised shower. She crawled fast against the wall and kept her knees and legs tight with her arms around them. Rostov drank half a glass of whiskey on the rocks like water, approached the woman again and grabbed her by the hair obligating the frightened woman to perform oral sex on him. Rostov ejaculated in her face; then shot her in the middle of the forehead with a 9 mm Beretta. As far as being worry about the loss, there was no reason to be worried; they never reported any prisoners taken to that location anyway.

In the morning, Major Hegedus ordered the male prisoners one by one to report to his office for interrogation. The main objective was to determine where Sheik Lazur almad Al-Fanistar was hidden because intelligence reports concluded that this one might be close by and with Osama bin Laden planning several terrorist attacks in Europe and in the United States.
The first man told Hegedus in his face: "Fuck You and Die!!" according to Mussad Yanir, a Lieutenant with the new Iraqi Police force attached to the regiment in Afghanistan as a translator. Major Hegedus punched the prisoner in the face so hard that the prisoner started bleeding through his nose; the victim continued to shout in his native language "Fuck you and die" to Major Hegedus who opened a bottle of Tabasco sauce from one of his MRE packages and pour about an ounce of it in the victim's nose. He ordered Yanir to handcuff the victim and to take him back to his cell. The bloody man screamed so loud that the other prisoners

knew what kind of interrogation was awaiting them. Next, Major Hegedus wanted to try with a female. A young lady was brought in the office and she was ordered to seat in the chair placed in the middle of the room. Hegedus asked through the translator: "Where is the Sheik?..If you tell me where he is, I promise you that I'll let you go right now to your family……, so tell me....Where is him?" The lady responded: Maybe in Kastan. The Major looked into her eyes about one and a half inches from her face and said: "That means, he still there?", and the lady responded: "That is the only place he has ever been". Hegedus abandoned the room and went to an adjacent office where members of a Delta Force team where processing more information for the special-forces platoons near Kastan and informed them of this new revelation. Hegedus entered back to the interrogation room and gave the woman a kiss in the right cheek, and told her: "You are free to go". Yanir was ordered to give the woman a ride back to Szakistan. She never made it to the camouflaged vehicle. One bullet penetrated the back of her head at the doorsteps of Major Hegedus' office, while this one was securing his 9 mm Beretta back in his right holster.

Eleven minutes after the information was given to the Delta Forces, a group of twelve Special Forces were already in the air aboard Black Hawk 45HK2. The lead man was Lieutenant Hinca, a Colombian-American officer veteran of the Panama Invasion and the Persian Gulf War, who also earned the purple heart in Somalia and the Medal of Valor after seizing a terrorist compound in Shala-Balag rescuing two American soldiers that were hostages at that location. The coordinates were given in the air, and the drop zone was half a mile from the only visible village through satellite pictures.

Six terrorists were attentive inside foxholes with shoulder launchers as they protected the Sheik from any attack. When the Black Hawk was in sight, two of the terrorists fired a missile at once spreading hot pieces of metal, flesh and blood through the purple sky of Kastan. A ten-man team drove the Sheik to a secured place underground about four miles West of Kastan. The Sheik informed about the raid to Alfad Dal Kaden, who was reading the newspaper at Heathrow Airport in London waiting for his flight to Montreal.

Major Hegedus was furious about the loss and ordered to execute the rest of the prisoners one by one and have them to look how they eliminate their comrades. He never knew that in fact the Sheik was there and that he was transported to a safer place. All he knew was that the female he killed sent the troops to an ambush. The Sheik was in a secluded area located west of Kastan and about sixty miles from where Osama bin Laden was hiding. The Sheik sent one of his messengers to see Osama to aware him about the situation and to receive further orders if any in regards to their strategy. A day after, the messenger returned to inform the Sheik that no changes would be made. They just regrouped and continued with the plan.

At the Mozak camp, Sergeant Glen Rostov was making sure that the remaining of the prisoners were executed one by one. They all were eliminated and their bodies cremated. That was the end of the unknown prisoners.

A few days later Sheik Lazur almad Al-Fanistar advised Osama bin Laden that Alfad Dal-Kaden was already in New Jersey after flying from Teheran to London, then to Montreal and from this one to Newark with an Egyptian passport. Alfad was the key element for the next attack in American soil and both Osama and the Sheik wanted it to be a successful event. They were orienting their tactics to areas were the guard was low instead on focusing in areas were the Americans think they are going to be hit again, which is stupid, illogical, and against all strategies of war.

Also, Osama's security advisors were already planning to execute a sensitive move, the secure and successful relocation of Osama and his top advisors to another location.
The next location for Osama's headquarters was a cave located fifty miles east of Kjanajastan between the spider mountains and the main road that access Kabul from the north. The relocation was to take place around 4 am, which was the best time to execute operations like this after studying well the coalition forces state of alertness during the night. The morning of the execution of the plan, Osama was wearing a bullet-proof vest under his white and long garment and he was hidden in the back of a semi-armored white van, riding in it with four heavily armed bodyguards. Behind the van, a pickup truck with three individuals, one at the wheel, one in the passenger seat with and automatic weapon, and one in the back with grenade launcher and a rocket-missile device, and behind the pickup truck another pickup truck with a driver and two mercenaries in the back of it, carrying an M-60 submachine gun, and a SAW machine gun, both stolen weapons from American victims. In front of the white van and as the scout team, a Nissan Titan 4x4 with three heavily armed terrorists that were opening the path for the upcoming vehicles. The operation didn't last much and everybody was transferred to the cave safely.
Osama bin Laden knew that transfers like this are to be often due to the fact that he declared war against America and jumping from place to place will allowed him to see how good the American intelligence community were in disseminating new information regarding tracking him down and if they were capable to do so. So

far, up to the present time it still is a complete mess and Osama still at large for over seven years.

Major Hegedus was preparing an official ceremony for the burial of the victims of the Black Hawk led by Lieutenant Hinca. Several locals attended the ceremony and were shouting anti-Taliban words in support for the American troops and the cause for their liberation and prosperity. In a brief speech to the multi-national troops, Hegedus stated: "...this is making me stronger and more appreciative about life, but it will never make me and it will never make all of us weak, unresponsive, and inefficient when dealing with the enemy. We still are alive and we have a mission to do, and we will accomplish it until we shut down every single cave that shelters terrorists, and we will eliminate them from the face of the Earth".

Sheik almad Al-Fanistar received a call from Alfad dal-Kaden upon his arrival to Newark International Airport. He was told by the spiritual leader that a man by the name of Farsal was waiting for him at the luggage pick-up area with a sign that reads: Atlantic Company. Sure he was. Alfad immediately made eye contact with Farsal, they shook hands and went to the parking area were a black Lincoln Continental was the mean to transport him to the Plaza Sixty Hotel in Manhattan, New York. The driver told Alfad that the next morning he was picking him up from the hotel for a long drive; a ten hours drive south on I-95 to North Carolina, as ordered by the Sheik.

The circle of trust among terrorist is tide, especially if all orders where coming from the spiritual leader. They learn to follow orders and to experience at first hand multiple changes and different strategies that appear without notice, and they were efficient in learning and executing them.

Sheik Lazur almad Al-Fanistar contacted Hajak in Tampa, Florida to advised him that the leader of the operation was en route to North Carolina and that shortly he will be arriving to Florida for the reunion and revision of the plan to follow. Hajak gave the news to professor Sahkir who was making a presentation at the University of Tampa.

The security forces of Osama bin Laden were in a meeting addressing him about the different perspectives of the war to include the news that were on the air in London, Tel-Aviv, Montreal, Washington, and Iraq. None of them were the same when compared to each other. Also, as part of the dissemination evaluation intelligence process, the security forces filtered all these information presented to the public to analyze and compare it against the known reality to them in order to balance and determine the level of accuracy of what is said, the impact of it in the population as well as their response and support to the war against terrorism.

Osama knew that the majority of the American population did not support the war as they were doing so at the beginning of it. Thousands of innocent lives have been sacrificed and chaos still reigning in Baghdad, and there was no clue were Osama was hiding, just rumors that he was either in Afghanistan, Pakistan, Sudan, Yemen, Iran or in the same United States of America.

The security forces of the Sheik Lazur almad Al-Fanistar executed a recon of the area they were to pass in order to transport him to Osama's place for an important meeting about the mission. All the pieces were almost in position and it was the time to study the plan, make changes, analyze the objective, and finally execute the sacred mission. Early in the morning the masters of the plan reunited along with other important followers and advisors, while over fifty mercenaries surrounded the cave without been seen from a flat land equipped with portable missile launchers, M-60s, Kalashnikovs, and AK-47s. The Sheik placed on the dirt floor a map and many photographs of the objective, the Tampa Port, previously taken by the Kaljatahl group (Kadu, Hassan, Wadek, and Mardak) during their visit to the area aboard the Xanadu vessel. Copies of the same documents were given to Alfad dal-Kaden while ridding comfortably in the black Lincoln Continental on his way to North Carolina by Farsal, the driver, as instructed by the Sheik.

While Alfad was reviewing the documents and getting familiar with the objective, Osama bin Laden was also learning about it.
Osama wanted the complete destruction of the port by initiating the attack towards the oil reservoirs, neutralizing rescue by also destroying the adjacent bridges with explosives detonated via cellular phones. He wanted a huge cloud of smoke and fire to invade the skies of the Gulf of Mexico to distract the attention from the northeastern part of the American nation to the southwest region of it. As he mentioned before in several of his meetings, attacking America is like playing a video game, he has the remote control in his hands and fires the enemy when he wants, as many rounds as he wants, and then turn the game off when he does not want to play anymore. American strategists also feel that way, especially when there is a long period of silence not knowing when the next attack is going to take place and where it could be.

Farsal, the driver of the black Lincoln Continental proceeded with the instructions previously given by the Sheik and told Alfad Dal-

Kaden that he was taking him to Raleigh International Airport to catch a flight to Jacksonville, Florida. Farsal asked the passenger for all his documents and anything else he used in Europe prior to his flight from London to the United States. In exchange, Farsal gave him a manila envelope containing one thousand dollars in cash and a Florida driver's license identifying him as Gabriel Rahid while in the United States.

Farsal called the Sheik to let him know that Gabriel Rahid was already aboard American Airlines flight 256 en route to Jacksonville. This event was communicated to Osama bin Laden who ordered the Sheik to call Sheik Balad Ramal Rayid alamh al-Marharad who resides in Jacksonville for the pick-up time and transport of the leader to the western part of the state of Florida. Both Sheiks had a conversation and everything was working fine and on the clock.

The security forces posted outside the cave where the masters of the plan were reunited detected three vehicles driving north on one of the adjacent dirt roads to the cave area. The striking team composed of ten heavily armed terrorists approached the vehicles about a mile from the red zone, the zone of the meeting. They ordered the occupants to get out of the vehicles and placed them on the ground to be searched. They were regular citizens going from one side of the town to the other aboard stolen vehicles as they confessed but with no interest in fighting any type of war. The lead man ordered the execution of the six men and two children immediately. They couldn't risk anything when protecting Osama bin Laden. As they regrouped back to their initial position, the lead man excused himself and entered the cave to report the event. The Sheik kissed the man in the cheek before he left the cave back to his security duties.

Osama and the Sheik were also determining their next hidden place in order to continue with the objective and many other plans to attack the United States, Israel and some other places in Europe.

Hours later the security forces of Sheik Lazur almad Al-Fanistar escorted him back to his place on the west side of Kastan, while Osama stayed for a couple more days at his location. The American Airlines flight 256 arrived at 8 pm at Jacksonville International Airport, and an envoy from Sheik Balad Ramal was already in place waiting for Gabriel holding a sign that reads: Atlantic Company. Alfad dal-Kaden walked to the luggage pick-up area and saw a short chubby man holding the sign, approached him and saluted him in Spanish: "Hola amigo, estamos listos para irnos?" and the chubby driver responded: "Vamonos amigo, gusto de conocerlo". Both men walked a short distance to the blue Nissan X-Terra in the parking garage; prior to get in the vehicle, the chubby man handled Gabriel a large bulky envelope as instructed by Sheik Balad Ramal. The vehicle took off and they were en route to Tampa, Florida. Gabriel opened the envelope and found a cell phone with a note attached to it to call Sheik Lazur almad Al-Fanistar to a different number, a small envelope containing three hundred dollars and two rolls of quarters. Gabriel called the Sheik to report his safe arrival to Jacksonville and told him that he was a little exhausted of too many trips. The Sheik told him that in Tampa he will meet with people trained at his old school back in Iran. The Sheik also mentioned that American intelligence agents recorded Alfad's death in their system and that as far as they are concerned, Alfad Dal-Kaden was dead. Gabriel responded: "Is nice to come back to life". The chubby driver did not have any clue of what was going on. He was the only person that drove Alfad, now known as Gabriel without knowing anything about the plot.

The driver was nice and courteous with the passenger. They stopped in a fast food restaurant to buy some chicken burgers and fries with a large smoothie for Gabriel, then at a gas station to fill up; while the driver was putting some gas into the vehicle, Gabriel entered the market to purchase a box of large cigars. Back inside the vehicle, Gabriel contacted professor Sahkir to let him know that he will be in Brandon in the next two hours. Sahkir gave him instructions to stop by the Red Roof Inn located out of I-75 on Route 60 and to go straight to Room 320 where he will be waiting for him. The driver was advised and agreed to drop Gabriel off at that hotel.

Gabriel contacted again Sheik Lazur almad Al-Fanistar to ask him about the arrangements for the Kaljatahl group. The Sheik informed him that he already contacted them in India and that the next shipment was scheduled in two weeks, meaning that they will be arriving at the port in month and a half or less, enough time for Gabriel to recon the area with the professor and Hajak, one of his old students in Iran who also believes him dead.

Sheik Lazur contacted Osama bin Laden to inform him about the events. Osama told him that he is in the process of moving to Jarak, 60 miles west of his position to the small village of the same name where him and Lazur used to spend time of prayers during the Iran-Iraq conflict.

The security forces protecting Osama bin Laden were regrouped in three teams, the recon team, the protection team, and the support team. The recon team formed by six elements left the cave area around 5 am on a cold Wednesday morning and they moved west and northwest for about five miles and returned to the cave to lead the convoy after detecting no problem on their way.

Osama was wearing one more time the bullet proof vest under his dirty white garment and got in the semi-armored white van along with four guards, followed by two pick up trucks with four terrorist each fully armed. A few meters behind the support forces with two other pick-up trucks with M-60 and portable missile launchers. Surprisingly, there were no confrontations with the coalition forces or any resistance force in the region. One more time, Osama bin Laden was in a different location and safe. Jarak became the command post for all terrorist operations of Al Q'aeda. The Sheik announced that the plan was ready, the men were ready, and that their spirits were also ready.

TAMPA, FLORIDA, USA
"The Execution Plan"

The blue Nissan X-Terra was going 95 miles per hour on a deserted 60 miles per hour rural road going west across the Florida Turnpike without realizing that they were spotted by State Trooper Hudgins. The chubby driver noticed in his rear view mirror the approaching black and tan Chevrolet Caprice that just turned on the lights and sirens. Gabriel was a little nervous but in control. Officer Hudgins made another normal routine stop and after getting the driver's license and registration went back to his cruiser. The chubby man knew that the Officer was writing a ticket. He got it. The chubby driver apologized to the officer who never took his dark glasses off. The officer simply walked away and stayed in his patrol vehicle until the chubby man took off. Gabriel reached to the back seat were his handbag was located and got one hundred and fifty dollars for the driver to pay the ticket as an appreciation for the inconvenience. The driver was satisfied.

About forty minutes before they entered Brandon, they made a stop at a gas station owned by a Moroccan family to buy some coffee, the newspaper, and some gum. Gabriel heard them talking in their native language and didn't doubt in joining the conversation. The owner was amazed to share exciting moments with an unknown visitor at least for a couple minutes. The chubby man grabbed two hot-dogs from the rusty revolving rack and a bottle of soda. Gabriel paid for everything and left the store. The chubby driver, concentrated in the two hot-dogs did not paid attention to the only street light in the little village and drove through the red light. Unfortunately, a patrol vehicle was approaching the intersection and saw the running blue Nissan. Officer Hass stopped the vehicle. Again lights and sirens were behind the X-Terra; this time the chubby man asked the officer to let them go. The officer asked both men to exit the vehicle and to approach his cruiser.

The strong odor of the cheap cigars tricked the officer, who after verifying that it was from a cigar let the men back into the vehicle. He wrote the ticket and the chubby man signed it. A few minutes later they were in Brandon en route to the hotel to meet with the professor and Hajak.

The chubby man parked the vehicle by the pool in the rear section of the hotel and helped Gabriel with the luggage. At this time, Gabriel thanked the man for the adventurous driving across Florida and told him to be careful when driving back to Jacksonville. The chubby man left and Gabriel's steps on the stairwells sounded tired but decisive. At the door of room 320, the professor received Alfad Dal-Kaden and invited him in.

A few minutes later, Hajak entered the room and he almost fell on the floor when he saw Alfad sitting on one of the two queen beds.

This was the first time they saw each other since the supposed dead of Alfad in Iran when Hajak and the other members of the Kaljatahl group were training for the operation in the United States and they even went to his funeral.

The atmosphere inside the room changed and the low volume on the television set was ignored when they started praying to thank the Almighty for the continuous success of the plan, for their safety, and for their cause. The men cheered with cognac and talked a little bid about the good and bad things about the training camp in Iran. Alfad told the men why he planned his dead, and also told them that it was part of the plan as ordered by Sheik Lazur almad Al-Fanistar years ago. Alfad told the men that his new identity was Gabriel Rahid and asked them to start addressing him as Gabriel and to get used to his temporary new life in the United States. Hajak was concerned, as well as professor Sahkir for the reward posted years ago by the FBI of two hundred thousand dollars for tips leading to the capture of Alfad Dal-Kaden for his presumable participation in the bombings of the American embassies in Kenya and Tanzania and for his ties with Osama bin Laden and frequent trips to India to negotiate with members of the Al Yamat terrorist organization. Gabriel explained, that intelligence reports from several Islamic organizations around the world have expressed their satisfaction to know that the American intelligence community, Department of State, FBI, CIA, NSA, and several security departments at different American embassies around the globe have put an end to the manhunt of Alfad dal-Kaden giving plenty consideration and trust to his fabricated death. However, Islamic intelligence reports have detected that certain members of the Israeli Mossad, in support to the American counterintelligence never close the case and that they might be searching for Alfad everywhere in the world. Therefore, Gabriel was still a target and he must not remain in one place for extended periods of time. Gabriel disclosed to the attentive men that the Kaljatahl group was scheduled to arrive a little over a month aboard a Greek vessel bringing dry cement to American Python Company. According to the Sheik's instructions, he continued, the group was ready to abandon their duties on the day of the attack, a day without a date and time still.

The three men had only one month to recon the area, gather all the necessary information collected by Hajak and the professor during the past months to include the rental of a helicopter for tourism and a small plane for low altitude flight along the bay with the intentions to hijack it and redirected it towards the oil reservoirs at the port that run parallel to 21st Street with no security at all but a 6 foot fence; the evaluation of police presence in the area, the access control procedures dictated by the port authority under the control of personnel from a private security company, the easy access and movement inside the port, and everything in relation to the routes of escape if the situation would allow them to do so, otherwise they were committed to die for the cause before being captured, as also ordered by the Sheik and Osama bin Laden.

It was getting late and Sahkir and Hajak wanted to leave the new leader alone so he can shower and go to bed. They agreed to meet in the morning for breakfast. The professor indicated that he will be back by 8 am to pick up the new guest, and immediately left the place with Hajak.

Gabriel took a shower and prepared a cup of coffee while arranging several paper work, maps, notes, and news clips to read and evaluate the strategy to be utilized for a successful terrorist attack. The television set volume was low while a CNN reporter was talking from Baghdad reporting the death of three US Marines ambushed right outside the school that was utilized to store the boxes to be used for the ballots during the next presidential elections. A car bomb was detonated via cellular phone when the militaries where approaching the area in a camouflaged vehicle.

Gabriel was more concentrated on the papers on top of his desk but heard something of the broadcasting and redirected his attention for brief seconds to the screen just to feed a little more his sarcasm about the loss of American troops. For the next three hours he designed two different strategies and named them as plan Raj and plan Jehj. The first one was oriented towards an immediate air strike of the oil reservoirs, and the second to the neutralization of power supply to the port followed by an immediate detonation of multiple bombs previously placed in several key points. His major concern was not the security of the port since it is well known by all the intelligence reports processed by Hajak and professor Sahkir for the past several months that it is minimum, non-security oriented and that the personnel assigned had no clue at all of what real security is all about. They also knew that any MARSEC (Maritime Security) Level increase is nothing but an increase in personnel instead of security quality.

Gabriel decided to continue in the morning and went to sleep. In the morning, around 7 am, he telephoned professor Sahkir who told him to be ready in one hour to go out for breakfast. Around that time, the professor and Hajak picked up Gabriel and went to a McDonald's on Adamo Street. They actually ordered like six big breakfasts, two for each hungry man. They sat close to the east window and started eating right away. Gabriel disclosed to them the two possible plans of attack and they all agreed to go with the Plan Raj. Two minutes of silence followed while they were devouring the sausages and hash browns; in the meantime, Hajak observed through the window that in the parking lot there were two big fat cops from the Hillsborough County Sheriff, a black male and a blonde female. Hajak told Gabriel that cops usually frequent places like McDonalds and Dunkin Donuts for breakfast, lunch or dinner, and that they like to be in groups, and that their level of alertness is minimum. Police officers in America, he proceeded, are not seekers, they are wait-to-happen in order to respond to any situation from minor to major crimes, and none of them are terrorism oriented or trained to the level of prevention and counter-attack. The only difference between a regular private security guard and a police officer is the time in school, and the power of enforcing the law, he concluded. Gabriel didn't care much about the police because he already knew that police officers are not an element of discouraging any of his plans due to the fact that they are bodies in the streets as any other civilians.

After twenty minutes of short talking and a lot of food, the men abandoned the establishment and walked to the white van that already had the magnet sign that reads: "Atlantic Environmental Services" the same that was parked next to one of the patrol vehicles. Gabriel saluted the officers in a military manner and the black man responded in the same way with a sympathetic smile. The men got in the van and drove away going west on Adamo Street. At the traffic light in the intersection of Adamo Street and 22nd Street, the van turned right towards 7th Avenue. The driver, professor Sahkir showed Gabriel the typical enchants of Ybor City, and told him that before the day was over they were coming back for some good pizza and beer.

Driving down south on 21st Street, the van was en route to terminal 7 at the port of Tampa. Professor Sahkir and Hajak showed their orange port identification badges reflecting the name of their non-existent company, while Gabriel was covered in the back of the van with several sheets full of paint and several debris and tools. The van was never searched by the almost seventy years old private security officer who wrote on the clipboard that the van was going to American Python for their regular weekly services.

For the past three months, once a week and in some opportunities twice a week, the Atlantic Environmental white van was well known by the private security officers at the main entrance of one of the most vulnerable points of entry to our nation. Hajak and Sahkir were always polite and sometimes brought coffee for the officers. They always noticed that the port authority officers were never attentive to the entrance and control of the access point to the port; instead, they were most of the time gathered at the office located at the left area of the gates. The two identification badges were real, the company was false, the van was never searched, the tenant was never contacted to verify the services, and one individual entered without an identification badge and never spotted either.

When inside the port, the van just rode wherever its occupants wanted to go. They took a look at the several companies inside while Gabriel was writing their names down; they observed no security at all at the companies' entrances and they spotted only two pick-up trucks with port authority officers going around without having suspicion of anything wrong. They stopped briefly at berth 519 from where they can easily see the private airport across the bay. They continued their ride and passed by the Amoco, Marathon, and Shell combustible reservoirs without being challenged by anybody. Gabriel noticed that the same white pick-up truck belonging to the port authority was also patrolling that area raising no suspicion at all about their driving without destiny inside the port. Gabriel knew it was the same truck because he wrote the numbers showed on the yellow license plate in his agenda. He also took pictures of several points inside the port. They drove by the railroad tracks and noticed that certain tankers were the means of transportation for some toxic chemicals and that those tankers were adjacent to the road without any barriers, security or cameras monitoring the area. Upon leaving the port, Gabriel was amazed that there was no security inspection or checks upon leaving and for instance, he concluded that there was no security auditing done at all by the upper security clowns of homeland security.

The van was going west on Adamo Street and the magnetic sign was already removed. They were en route to Sahkir's office at the University of Tampa. The van was parked on the north side at the main faculty building and the corresponding parking permit was placed on the rear view mirror. All three men walked inside the building and their walking cadence on the wooden floors resembled the ones on the torn, dirty and uneven wooden floors in one of the classrooms back in Teheran.

Inside Sahkir's office, Gabriel was shocked by the tall American flag set on a stand on the right corner of it; he walked towards it and with an uncontrollable hatred said to himself: "Little by little all the stars are going to vanish and I'm here to make it happen..." Sahkir abruptly interrupted him by saying: "You cannot let your instincts act like this, not in here". The professor also indicated that he wasn't pleased either to have the American flag inside his office since it was in every single office as the facility's policy. He called for a drink and served the men a glass of cognac. They sat around the round table usually used for meetings. That was a meeting anyway, but not with educational purposes. From the balcony, they could see areas of the port and some areas of the small airport by using the telescope placed in the balcony. Gabriel downloaded all the pictures previously taken at the port by using Sahkir's computer. Then, he printed all of them. Hajak and the professor were amazed of Gabriel's ability to take pictures in sequence making really easy to place them side by side and have a big picture like if it was an aerial photograph of the area.

All photos were placed on top of the table and analyzed in detail especially the roads leading to the combustible reservoirs, entrances, fences, and berths. The meeting last for a couple hours and then the men abandoned the building aboard the white van. Gabriel made a call to Sheik Lazur almad Al-Fanistar to give him an update of the activities and to inform him of the Plan Raj. The Sheik gave him his blessings and supported the strategy as it was the best alternative as previously wished by Osama bin Laden too.

Sheik Lazur also informed Gabriel about the preparation for a new attack in London and Bali and that they might need his services for the direction of the operations in Bali right after the Tampa attack.

Sheik Lazur said that Al Q'aeda's intelligence branch was just waiting for the intelligence reports from several cells already operating in that area. The offer was an exciting opportunity for Gabriel who never doubted in cooperating with the cause.

The men went back to the Red House Inn were Gabriel was staying and decided to hang in there for a couple hours watching the news and reading the newspaper. Gabriel called for some food delivery and they ordered chicken wings, garlic rolls and sodas. About forty minutes later the food was placed on the round table inside the room and the men ate with so much enthusiasm that there was nothing left but clean bones. Professor Sahkir and Hajak left around 4 pm while Gabriel was ready for a nap until 6 pm. They decided to get together about 9 pm for dinner at a pizza place in Ybor City. The white van left the parking lot for the rest of the afternoon.

Later on at night the same white van was entering the parking lot and Gabriel was already attentive to it, descending the stairwells with charm, wearing some black Ralph Laurent pants, and an aqua-marina Zegna sporty shirt. The three men left towards Ybor City. Sahkir never forgot to place his 9 mm Beretta under the driver's seat before getting out of the vehicle, and after doing so, the combatants were walking west on 7th Avenue browsing through the stores, bars and cafes. While sitting at one of the pizza parlors, Gabriel got a call from Sheik Lazur almad Al-Fanistar who just woke up to inform that the Kaljatahl group was scheduled to be at the port the following Wednesday, a week earlier from the initial date.

The men celebrated with beer and pizza one of the last nights together before they concentrated in full to the operation. Professor Sahkir told Hajak and Gabriel about the plans to rent a small plane with the supposedly intentions to flight low across the bay using ten additional men from the university as a tourist group to avoid suspicions instead of just renting the plane himself. He already planned the flight with ten students who did not have the idea that the professor's intentions where of immolation in the name of the Almighty and against the evil force of capitalism.

Hajak picked up the bill and then they continued to walk west on 7th Avenue and entered one the famous strip bars in the area. It didn't take that long for Gabriel to get desperate for Shantal, a famous blonde stripper who lap danced in one of the private boots giving him oral sex for a couple hundred dollars, while the other two men just enjoyed the view of the live sex theater where three girls were performing several sex acts. After a couple hours of lascivious experiences, their instincts called for more celebration for the fall of the stars of the American flag, one by one as stated during their stay at the professor's office in the University of Tampa. The combatants left the establishment and walked a couple blocks before they got to their vehicle. The night was over and they got to their places to rest. The following morning they were to meet to analyze and review the final steps of the plan.

The television set turned on by itself around eleven o'clock in the morning, and Gabriel heard the mumble of a cartoon episode. He realized that it was time to get up, so he reached for the phone to call the professor. They both agreed to meet at two o'clock in the afternoon at the hotel. The professor and Hajak brought with them all the paperwork and information pertaining to the plan to start the final reviews of it as a group.

Once in the hotel, the professor announced that he already had the ten men group to fly with him the day of the hit and that on Monday morning he was going to reserve a plane for a tentative date; Hajak announced that the fabrication of one thousand pounds of explosive was already done and packed and ready to be loaded into a twenty-four footer truck to be rented from Ryder and that the truck was to be parked nearby the railroad tracks parallel to the combustible reservoirs and the tanks of toxic and flammable gases. The explosives will be packed in moving boxes and labeled as books and clothing. Gabriel announced that the white van will be loaded with C4 and parked in the parking lot by the Port Authority main building.

They concluded that the Kaljatahl group will load and set one hundred pounds of C4 inside the arriving vessel; the group members would leave the ship as normal daily routine and upon returning they will be in possession of plastic bags with boxes of audio equipment simulating shopping items, but full of explosives. Each of the four members of the group, Kadu, Wadek, Mardak, and Hassan were to rent four SUV's from four different locations and take the vehicles to an area nearby Brandon where hundreds of pound of explosives and chlorine barrels were stored inside a house-ranch of an eighty-five years old Muslim combatant by the name of Mohamed Sistani who was also a very close friend of Hajak. All four SUVs were to be parked in key locations to be disclosed later on and detonated via cell phones covering an extensive area of the port, especially the routes that access this facility. Wednesday was one day ahead and the combatants went to bed early right after eating at a local Italian restaurant in Brandon.

In the morning, the professor took Hajak to Ryder where they rented the truck needed for the operation then they drove it to a village right outside of exit 250 on I-75, where Mohamed was waiting for them to load it with the already fabricated explosives made from fertilizers. It was ten o'clock in the morning, and Hajak stayed at the ranch with the truck while the professor was en route to the hotel to meet with Gabriel. At the ranch, Mohamed utilized the help of five of his workers, four of them Muslims and one Mexican who thought they were loading barrels of mulch and dirt to be taken to another ranch nearby. Professor Sahkir arrived at the hotel after a twenty minutes ride and met with Gabriel who was already waiting for him to go out for some breakfast. They went to the local Denny's on Route 60 and started to made checks to the list of things-to-do and kept tracking of all movements. At this time, Gabriel called Sheik Lazur almad Al-Fanistar to inform him that the plan Raj was going well and that they were expecting the arrival of the vessel coming from Greece by four o'clock in the afternoon. The Sheik gave them his blessings in the name of the Almighty and stated his satisfaction with the status of the plan; he mentioned that he was to get in touch with Osama bin Laden, who was already involved in the planning of some terrorist attacks in Bali. The two combatants were eating t-bone steaks and eggs with coffee and reviewing again every single step of the plan and analyzing the probabilities of changes if any trouble or suspicion arises while following it. After breakfast, they stopped by the hotel and watched the news and relaxed a little bit until one o'clock in the afternoon. In the meantime, Hajak was almost done with the loading and now he was in the process to verify that all connectors and detonators were in place and ready to be activated. He made contact with professor Sahkir and decided to have lunch around three o'clock at Mohamed's ranch; the professor offered them to buy lunch from a local restaurant for the entire crew.

Sahkir and Gabriel went to Publix supermarket and stopped by the prepared-food section and they ordered nine lunch boxes of yellow rice, chicken stew, and yucca along with nine 20 oz. bottles of coke. They drove to the ranch and met with all the combatants for lunch. They also drank some cognac to celebrate for the upcoming plan; the Mexican guy knew there was a celebration of something but he never understood the language; he just ate like a pig and drank the very expensive cognac. Around four o'clock, professor Sahkir placed the magnets on the van that read Atlantic Environmental Services, and left the property along with Gabriel and Hajak en route to the port.

Sheik Lazur almad Al-Fanistar called Gabriel to inform him that Captain Altaraban Ghandaran was in command of the Xanadu vessel arriving from Greece as he did in his previous delivery. The captain was a loyal supporter of Al Q'aeda, Al Yamat and to the entire Islamic community on behalf of the destruction of Israel and the capitalism in the world. His supportive role in the operation was to concede the passes for the members of the Kaljatahl group to leave the ship and to return as they pleased while the rest of the crew was dedicated in full to the operations related to the disembark of 50,000 tons of dry cement to the silos of American Python Company located at berth 519.

The white van approached the main entrance to the port and the combatants were greeted by a sixty some years old private security officer who wrote the badge numbers belonging to Hajak and Sahkir, but he never noticed or bother to check the back of the van where Gabriel was actually hiding. In matter of seconds, they were inside and en route to berth 519. They drove by and noticed that the Xanadu vessel was already docking and decided to stay in the area but not that visible since there were a lot of law enforcement presence to include FDLE, a jeep from the United States Customs, a van from the United States Coast Guard and a patrol vehicle belonging to the security personnel of American Python Company.

A few minutes later the combatants drove away and went to recon the already established points were they were supposed to park all vehicles with explosives for the grand day. A few minutes later, they stopped by the Seaman's Club and waited there for Captain Altaraban Ghandaran's call. The three men entered the club and ordered beers; in another table there were two port authority officers and a Lieutenant eating burgers and they never bothered or noticed that two of the three men that just entered the establishment possess port identification badges while the third one didn't have any or even a pass with him. If they did, they probably assumed that the pass or badge was left in the vehicle.

At the table, Gabriel verified one more time what Hajak and Sahkir had been telling him from the beginning, that nobody enforces anything and that their level of alertness is less than minimum. The combatants felt very comfortable and they never raised any suspicion. They were enjoying some beers and a basket full of French fries. Around five fifteen in the afternoon, Gabriel's phone rang; the call was from Captain Ghandaran stating that the government officials have left with the exception of two FDLE officers that parked their vehicles on the berth, and that there was a silver pick-up truck Ford F-150 with a security officer from American Python. The combatants were ready to meet their long-time combatants, friends and brothers in spirit, the Kaljatahl group. At this time, Gabriel told the professor and Hajak that he was taking full charge of the entire operation as per the Sheik's instructions.
They left the club en route to berth 519. The white van was stopped by Corporate Security Specialist George Nestor, a member of the port security team for American Python, who descended from his vehicle to process the visitors before boarding again.

He never bothered or noticed that Gabriel was hiding in the back of the van. Hajak, who was driving the vehicle, told the officer that he was there to pick up four crew members. While all this was happening, the two officers from FDLE (Florida Department of Law Enforcement) were chatting from their vehicles parked side by side leaving the access control duties in the hands of Security Specialist Nestor. A few minutes later, four men descended from the Xanadu vessel and they were processed accordingly by Officer Nestor. The van drove away with the Kaljatahl group with direction to Mohamed's ranch. They couldn't keep a low profile to express their gratitude and happiness of see each other again and for a good cause; they hugged and kissed each other over an over while saying some prayers of gratitude over and over until they got to the ranch.

At the ranch, Mohamed was introduced to the combatants. Professor Sahkir parked the white van adjacent to the Ryder truck and observed the surroundings and he couldn't believe the fresh air he was breathing along with the successful step-by-step approach of the plan. He entered the house and he observed that on the table there was an almost empty bottle of cognac. Mohamed, Gabriel, Hajak, and the members of the Kaljatahl group Wadek, Mardak, Hassan and Kadu were holding a glass of cognac and professor Sahkir took only one second to join them for the cheering of such an important plan. This was the first time that the main eight participant members of the terrorist attack to be executed were together. After the drinks, they sat on a long table where they were about to share some bread, fried fish, rice and wine. During dinner, Gabriel took the lead and thanked all the men for their courage and announced to them on behalf of Osama bin Laden and Sheik Lazur almad Al-Fanistar how the plan was to be handled and their individual roles along with an alternate plan for each member in the event that something goes wrong. The aftermath of the plan was to successfully detonate the explosives in the selected key points of the port, the successful hijack of a rented small plane followed by the crashing of it on the combustible reservoirs, and the successful detonation of vehicles outside the port to delay the assistance to the inside victims.

Captain Ghandaran received a call from the Sheik who informed him about the part of the plan never disclosed to him until then. Sheik Lazur told the Captain that the day of the attack he was to leave the vessel since it was to be loaded with explosives also. Ghandaran agreed to leave the embarkation when it was necessary and he was advised that he was under the orders of Gabriel, the old friend and leader known in Iran as Alfad Dal-Kaden.

After dinner, Gabriel placed on the table all photos taken in the port and gave each comrade copies of all the steps to take for a successful plan. The coordination of events was a key element to distract the law enforcement and emergency agencies.

Gabriel announced all the steps. Professor Sahkir was responsible to take Kadu, Hassan, Wadek, and Mardak to Tampa International Airport so they can rent the vehicles from Budget, Enterprise, and Avis the day before the attack. After renting the vehicles with their own credit cards, they were to drive to the ranch where Mohamed had instructions to load the vehicles with explosives and to stay at that location waiting for further instructions. Right after the airport, professor Sahkir was also responsible to rent the plane as part of a University group of students going on a tourism trip over the bay. The final destination was the immolation of this loyal combatant against the combustible reservoirs. Hajak was responsible to park the Ryder truck in a key location while Gabriel picked him up in the white van.

After all vehicles loaded with explosives were in place, Gabriel and Hajak were to go and pick up Captain Ghandaran who previously was to assign tasks to the rest of the crew away from the area where the C4 boxes were to be put in place. All the men with the exception of professor Sahkir were to leave the port area and the surroundings in the white van.

Kadu, Hassan, Mardak and Wadek possessed a valid visa to enter the United States as well as Captain Ghandaran, Hajak and Gabriel. The two brothers, Hassan and Kadu were scheduled to leave the United States in a flight to Canada and then Turkey where they will meet with members of the Al Yamat to retreat for the Bali terrorist attack on schedule. Mardak and Wadek were scheduled to leave the United States about the same time to Frankfurt via Atlanta International Airport. Captain Ghandaran was scheduled to leave also via Atlanta International Airport to France. Hajak and Gabriel will stay in the United States but they will move from the Tampa area to south Florida. Gabriel and Hajak were the only two terrorists in charge of the phone calls that will detonate the explosives stored in the vehicles as scheduled.

The Kaljatahl group returned to the port late at night, and Security Specialist George Nestor processed them accordingly. The next morning, the same group would start bringing the boxes of C4 aboard and place them in strategic places of the vessel. The Xanadu vessel had four more days to finish the delivery of dry cement and Gabriel was aware of that so he can assess every step of the plan. At no time, law enforcement officers were concerned.

Professor Sahkir, Hajak and Gabriel were together at the local hotel and started praying for the upcoming days. Gabriel went to bed and Sahkir and Hajak left the hotel until the next morning.

The next day professor Sahkir announced to the ten students that everything was ready to go for the trip scheduled for Monday morning, a day with less visitors, and the best day in regards to the low profile of the authorities as established by pure observation throughout several months of quality surveillance done by Hajak. By eleven o'clock in the morning, Sahkir drove to the port to pick up the four combatants and took them to Tampa International Airport. Kadu and Hassan went to Avis and they rented a Lincoln Continental and a Cadillac Escalade respectively; Wadek went to Enterprise Rental and got a Nissan Pathfinder; Mardak went to Budget and got a Chevrolet Van. The group left the airport one by one, as they were finishing with their respective vehicle rental transactions. By two o'clock in the afternoon, the entire group made it to Mohamed's place; by five o'clock, the vehicles were loaded with explosives and the combatants were ready for dinner. Professor Sahkir and Hajak stopped at a local barbecue place in Brandon and bought enough food for the combatants.

All the vehicles remained at the ranch for the next couple of days. In the meantime, professor Sahkir met with university authorities to reach an agreement for the release of the students going on a short trip above the bay. There were ten students, all of them Caucasian, seven males and three females. The team leader of the group was Jenny Schultz, an Austrian-American girl with strong aspirations to become an officer in the United States Army through the ROTC program, who was also very excited about the fun trip. During the evening hours of Sunday before Christmas, Gabriel called Sheik Lazur almad Al-Fanistar for the last blessings for the successful attack to come. The Sheik verified throughout intelligence information and all the set up steps of the attack plan that there was no room for failure.

The next morning, Monday before Christmas, around six o'clock in the morning, Hassan and Kadu showed up at the port main entrance in their own rented vehicles posing as a security guards coming on duty for Winter Forman Company and Pre-Fabricate of America Company respectively. The security officer at the main entrance, who was ready to be relieved by the incoming shift, simply recorded their names from their driver's licenses and did not process them with a pass. Upon entering the port, Kadu telephoned Gabriel to report their status and how the plan was developing. Kadu drove to the fenced area right across from Winter Forman and parked his vehicle loaded with explosives near the railroad tracks were seventeen tankers full with chlorine derivate liquids and gases were standing. He just remained in his vehicle reading the newspaper and saw the port authority vehicle patrolling the area two times in a two hour period. While all this was happening, Hassan went to an area on the north side of the Amoco combustible reservoirs and parked his vehicle loaded with explosives by the fenced area of Pre-Fabricated of America Company. Just a few yards on the other side of the fence and visible to the naked eye, there was an 8,000 gallons fuel farm. With these two vehicles the south-to-north fire strip was set and ready to be detonated.

Mardak drove his vehicle loaded with explosives inside the three levels parking garage right across from the cruises pier at the other side of the port. Wadek drove his vehicle loaded with explosives to the main entrance and parked it by the port authority main building; presumably to process his port identification badge as soon as the office opened for customer service. At this time, Gabriel was informed about the strategic positioning of the four combatants, the members of the Kaljatahl terrorist group.

At eight o'clock in the morning, professor Sahkir met with the group of students at the University's conference room near the library and shared with them moments of photographs taken by Jenny Schultz. Jenny, the leader of the group, immediately downloaded the pictures in her portable computer and e-mailed them to his family and friends. Professor Sahkir was waiting for Mr. Rodriguez, the driver of the campus' van to take them to the small airport right across American Python, on the other side of the bay. At the same time Gabriel was following Hajak who was driving the 24-footer Ryder truck towards the bridge right outside the entrance to Terminal-7.

Hajak parked the truck on top of the bridge on the southbound lane and set up all emergency lights and road blocks to pretend the truck just broke down; he also placed a cardboard sign on the dashboard indicating that help was on its way; this would alert police or bystanders and to prevent towing. A Hillsborough County Sheriff police car drove by and never bothered to stop to investigate the incident. Hajak jumped in Gabriel's van and went directly to the port. At the gate, Hajak who switched seats with Gabriel while this one hide on the back of the van as he always did it before, he was processed as Atlantic Environmental Services going to American Python Company. Once inside the port, they went to pick up Captain Ghandaran at berth-519. After that, they stopped by Winter Forman and Pre-Fabricated of America to pick up Kadu and Hassan. Minutes later, and on his way out, Wadek also joined them.

At the other side of the port, Mardak already took a taxi from the cruises pier terminal en route to Tampa International Airport to take a 9:30 flight. Hajak was also en route to the airport and get there on time to drop Hassan, Kadu, Wadek and Ghandaran.

Hassan and Kadu checked in for American Airlines flight 1100 en route to Canada with a final destination in Turkey. Mardak and Wadek checked in for Delta Airlines flight 256 to Atlanta with final destination in Frankfurt. Ghandaran's Continental flight 2287 to Atlanta with final destination in France was scheduled for 11:30 in the morning.

It was 10:15 in the morning and the Kaljatahl group was already in the air, Gabriel and Hajak drove in the professor's white van towards Ybor City and parked the vehicle in the south bound side of 7th Avenue between 25th and 26th Street. They hugged and kissed each other and prayed to the Almighty for victory. Gabriel called Sheik Lazur almad Al-Fanistar to inform him that the detonations call will be made immediately and that the combatants were safe and out of the area. The Sheik gave him the go ahead and hung up.

By 10:00 in the morning, the professor was already at the airport with the group of students for a short aerial tour along the Tampa Bay. Around 10:45, they were in the air and the professor called Gabriel to indicate that everything was on schedule and ready to proceed with the Raj Plan. There were no more calls to be received by Gabriel; just the enormous explosion ready to happen without knowing how the professor would hijack the plane and re-direct it straight to the combustible reservoirs.

Exactly at 11:00 am and after a struggle in the air, professor Sahkir managed to kill the pilot by injecting him on the neck with a venous substance with a small syringe that was hidden inside his video-camera handbag.

The adrenaline was high and the mission was the main and only objective in the professor's mind. This concludes the family values he built, his wife and family, his friends and worshippers at the mosque, his compromises with the education system at the University, and most of all, the compassion for those ten students that for a couple of years trusted him, enjoyed quality times in the classroom and looked at him as a mentor and as a leader.

Terrorism does not recognize normal values or peace and harmony; it encourages terror, panic, isolation, abuse, discomfort, hallucination, disaster, prepotency, disruption, and distrust.
Jenny Schultz felt all of that. She managed to call her mother without taking her phone to her sweaty ears; she just wanted somebody to listen to what could be her last moments alive, hoping to receive some divine help after seeing with her own eyes how a mentor became quickly an evil.

There were many thoughts that starting to accumulate in everybody's mind, to include the old jokes in the classroom when referring to the professor as "towel head" or possible satellite of Middle Eastern terrorism in the United States. It was too late for everything and for anything. The ten students were contemplating how the pilot was thrown to the floor and dragged outside the main cabin while all of them were forced to the back of the plane.
The call from the air came all the way to a small apartment in Temple Terrace. Jenny's father answered the call but the communication was not a regular one, it contained rare sounds and some screams. It called his attention even more because the caller identification device signaled his daughter's cellular phone. Mr. Schultz exclaimed: "Are you there Jenny...Jenny are you there?...Can you hear me?". A couple seconds later he decided to hang up hoping to wait for another call. It never came.

While checking their emails, Mr. and Mrs. Schultz retrieved the photo Jenny took before their departure to the flight of terror; they even made nice comments about the professor without knowing that he was part of the masterminding of a heinous terrorist plan about to happen.

Sahkir took immediate control of the small plane and threatened the students to crash it if they continue screaming. He pulled a handgun; a Beretta 9mm fully loaded and shot Lee Moco on his right calf, one of the male students who pretended to get close to the new Captain with intentions of becoming a hero. This event sent a warning signal to the rest of the students.
Sahkir change the course of the plane from its original northeast trajectory and started to go southwest towards the port of Tampa. He placed a final call to Gabriel and told him that he was going straight to the target. Gabriel waited to hear the explosion.

At this time, exactly at the 11 hour and 7 minutes, the fully gas-loaded plane crashed into the top center portion of one of the Amoco combustible reservoirs generating a huge explosion heard miles around. Gabriel and Hajak shout victory in the name of the Almighty immediately after the sound of the explosion generated a thick black cloud in the skies of one of the most beautiful cities in the State of Florida.

Gabriel and Hajak walked towards the parked van and started to leave the area before they heard any sound of sirens. While driving east on 7th Avenue, Gabriel made the first call that will detonate the explosives set inside the truck on top of the bridge. The call was made at the 11 hour and 9 minutes and the explosion damaged the entire bridge blocking any rescue access from the other side of it, paralyzing the efforts of suppressing the fire at the port.

Another call was made at the 11 hour and 10 minutes blowing in hundred of pieces the vehicle parked in front of Winter Forman, which its strategic positioning went even better of what initially was thought by the terrorist who were not sure if it would detonate the seventeen takers of chlorine derivate liquids and gases. It did. After two minutes of the initial explosion caused by the plane, the city of Tampa was witnessing one of the most evil attacks in history by international terrorists having as a background the initial and eternal noises of sirens from fire trucks, police vehicles, and ambulances.

The government of the United States failed one more time to secure its vital entries. The city of Tampa was the main victim; the port of Tampa was the chosen target; port security personnel, law enforcement individuals and homeland security experts were the puppets of the evil forces of terrorism one more time.

At the 11 hour and 14 minutes, just 7 minutes after the initial explosion, and during the first seconds of the arrival of the first responders to the cluster, another called detonated the vehicle parked by the fenced area of Pre-Fabricated of America Company. The adjacent 8,000 gallons of regular fuel blew up in the air in the blink of an eye. The inferno was imminent and help could not get into the nucleus of the volcano. Several fire trucks from the port itself were down due to the waves of the explosion, and some others could not go across the bridge because it was unsafe and blocked.

The few police cars and fire trucks that made it inside the port were actually entering the crater of an ambush. A final call made at the 11 hour and 19 minutes blew up the vehicle parked right outside the port authority main building.

The main gate was completely destroyed and on fire; the smoke was so thick in the air that nobody could see more than a couple feet in front. The Amoco reservoir fire suppression mechanism was completely immobilized and the explosion of the next reservoir was imminent.

Homeland security officials, fire marshals, police brass, and local government officials and emergency management personnel decided to set up an emergency command post by the cruises berth at the other side of the port. Governor Rick Bresh and his committee were notified of the incident by homeland security officials. A helicopter flanked by war planes was to bring Governor Bresh to the Command Post set up by homeland security officials. The white van was en route to the Florida turnpike heading towards Orlando.

By 12:30, the MARSEC level was elevated to Level-III and the national advisory was elevated to Red alert. Immediately after the changes, local authorities ordered the closing of all avenues towards the port of Tampa to include within ten miles radius. Fire Marshall and the US Coast Guard teamed up for the quick deployment of helicopters to suppress the fire from the air. The entry and exit of all vessels were immediately put on stand-by and the relocation of the closest vessels to the crater was ordered by the US Coast Guard. There was some confusion about the lead of the Command Post. At this time, entities' heads wanted to use their brains; one more time in America history, the terrorists were two steps ahead and government officials were two steps back thinking what to do next after the cluster fuck was already a matter of the international headline news.

At the 12 hour and 35 minutes, another call from the Kaljatahl group was made and it detonated the vehicle parked inside the garage across from the cruises pier, right above the Command Post. The explosion destroyed three levels of the garage and there were several people trapped inside, dead bodies all over the place, the streets were invaded by panic, cries, and desperation.

While heavy machines orange-colored were flying the air to suppress the fire, Gabriel and Hajak were entering a small town near Orlando where they checked in into a rural motel planning to stay the entire day watching the news. At the parking lot of the unpopular lodging place, Gabriel made his last call. It blew up the machine room of the Xanadu vessel sending millions of metal pieces in the air bringing down two helicopters from the US Coast Guard. The fire intensified and the chaos was enhancing the terror and diminishing the effectiveness of the homeland security circus.

It did not took long for the seventeen fuel trucks fully loaded parked inside the fenced area besides the Amoco reservoirs to be victims of the domino effect; they started to ignite one by one before the eyes of a worthless fire team that could not fight the fire; this was not the type of fire they were used to respond to, this was not the emergency situation they were trained for, the chaos and the panic went over the limits; it was another September 11 with a bay-view.
Fire Marshall Statham reunited at the Command Post with the State Homeland Security Director, Mr. John Shiff and with the

Tampa FBI Director, Mr. Mike Woodcall. The Department of Homeland Security issued an immediate order to close all airports and seaports in the State of Florida, and all airports in cities such as Atlanta, New Orleans, Raleigh, Austin, Houston, Denver, New York, New Jersey, Los Angeles, San Diego, Boston, Pennsylvania, and Chicago. For instance, all flights were cancelled until further notice and other airports were also forced to close and observe the emergency.

Upon arrival of Governor Rick Bresh, the Command Post was relocated inside a warehouse on Adamo Street very close to a railroad track. Major Renzo Nicca with the Hillsborough County Police Department utilized all his officers to block all avenues and streets as ordered by Homeland Security Officials. The burned bodies of dozens of port employees started to pile up and slightly observed by the cameraman from Channel-10 aboard the news channel helicopter.

The smell of burned combustible, the constant minor and major explosions without control, the chaos and unmanageable situation, and the increasing findings of charred victims were about to annihilate Mr. John Shiff who was experiencing chest pains. He was treated by some police officers and transported to the emergency room. Several high ranking officers of the US Coast Guard and US Customs and Border Patrol were playing the role they trained for: Nothing to do.

The nation's President was alerted about the chaos in Florida and the White House was ready to air a speech to the American public. One more time, the people of the United States of America had to be the loyal listeners of bad news. At a remote place near Orlando, two men were ready to hear the news too.

THE KALJATAHL TRIUMPH

Mr. and Mrs. Schultz made contact with the local FBI office by dialing the hotline showed on the televised breaking news. Their call was not answered immediately; it took thirty-five minutes. At the other end of the line, FBI agents heard it all, from suspicious vehicles to names of possible perpetrators, suspicious activities in residential communities in the past, tips of late meetings at different mosques, and even numerous tips targeting right-wing militias groups as the responsible parties. All leads needed to be analyzed. All tips were taken seriously and treated accordingly.

This call was different. Mr. Schultz reconfirmed that the plane that crashed against the Amoco combustible reservoirs was the one that was taking his daughter on a tour trip over the bay. Government officials were prompted to qualify this event as a terrorist attack. Mr. Schultz provided the list of the students aboard that flight and stated that he can provide a photo of the entire group prior to their departure to the premeditated inferno.

Television crew members were all over the Schultz' residence and all over the University of Tampa; they were trying to gather fresh and accurate information about their direct or indirect participation in the coward terrorist attack. The pressure was immense and the Schultz never thought that their residence would have more law enforcement officers than toothpicks in their kitchen cabinet. Mr. Woodcall and other FBI agents surrounded Mr. Schultz while he was accessing his computer to print the picture his daughter Jenny sent him via her cellular phone. Also, he mentioned to the bunch of brains that he received a call while she was on the air but that he never talked to her. She never hanged-up either, -as he explained- it is like she was trying her father to hear what was going on inside the plane.

The few pieces were put together and everything started to make a little more sense during the course of the investigation. The picture was printed. In the meantime, other FBI agents and Homeland Security officials run the background checks of all the students, the crew members and the professor.

Government authorities were eager to receive copy of the recorded call from the cellular company. It didn't take to long to determine that the event was in fact a terrorist attack orchestrated by Professor Sahkir, at least the aerial attack. His residence was ransacked by the FBI, his American wife arrested, and everything inside the house was tagged for investigation to include three personal computers, files, books, letters, two vehicles, and trash.

His photograph was aired on television and local law enforcement officials were asking for information that could help to understand the reason and course of the entire terrorist plan.
Several calls were received providing names of the Muslim community that were really close to professor Sahkir, names of campus employees and students that were close to him, and several other tips indicating the places he frequented before his suicidal mission.
Mr. Schultz made contact with several civilian organizations in order to raise some reward money for information about the terrorists or their facilitators.

In the meantime on national television, crew members of domestic and international press were reporting live from the outskirts of the Port of Tampa. Direct reporting was transmitted all over the world. The two combatants, Gabriel and Hajak, were enjoying the triumphant event in the name of the Almighty and minutes before they received the salute and admiration of Sheik Lazur Almad al-Fanistar and Osama bin Laden.

The plan was well organized and studied, but it didn't take much of a planning since the recon report revealed the unsatisfactory security in the area, the lack of conscious in the law enforcement officials, and the low preparation of all state and federal effectives.

A twenty-two year old blonde skinny girl knocked at the door of room 125 of the filthy motel and Gabriel received two boxes of sausage pizzas and a six-pack of coke; that was dinner for the night. They both were analyzing the results and recording all the necessary information such as flaws, mistakes, omissions, and successes.

Part of the plan required no communication at all of any type between up-line, down-line or lateral-line until the Sheik contacted Gabriel, the leader for further instructions. In Iran, Syria, London, and Canada there were counterintelligence units of Al Q'aeda and Al-Yamat terrorist organizations dedicating their time to analyze press released information from radio and television stations, internet blogs, and newspaper and magazine websites.

All the streets conducting to the Port of Tampa were closed. The traffic of vehicles on Adamo Street was restricted and several road blocks were implemented, vehicles were searched, by-standers were scrutinized before leaving the area, helicopters were conducting aerial patrol, and every official was moving. They didn't know what they were looking for. They didn't have any clue of the responsible of the attack. The Command Post had to be moved from the area where the cruises depart to the east side of Adamo Street in a warehouse by the railroad tracks. The Florida Department of Law Enforcement (FDLE) was conducting road blocks on I-75 north and south bounds. Vehicles were diverted to rest areas for inspection, every officer from the Florida Highway

Patrol was called to help and members of the American Red Cross were in place to provide water, food, medicine and any other type of assistance.

One of the most sensitive tasks in any criminal act regardless of its intensity is the preservation of the crime scene, the collection of evidence, photographing of the area, collection of information from witnesses or victims, and processing of suspects. The last one was a missing step.

Local news were limited to report from outside the port, nobody was actually allowed inside since firefighters, law enforcement, and homeland security officials were carefully entering as they were announcing the complete shut down of port activities and labeling the entire point of entry to the United States as a crime scene due to a major terrorist attack.

The FBI produced their first hot list for their investigation. It contained the names of the ten students and the professor from the University of Tampa, and the name of the pilot. Multiple teams were formed to target each person individually by going to their place of residence and interview as much persons as possible. All teams were armed with a search warrant. SWAT effectives visited the residence of the possible main suspect, professor Sahkir, along with FBI agents and reporters. They knew already about the professor's background, although no criminal record in the United States, they just didn't follow procedures for not stereotyping individuals just because their origin, nationality or religion, for example. They just didn't like that among the group there was a Muslim man.

The FBI counterterrorism team agents collected a couple of glasses with residue of cognac from the professor's office at the university. Ouch! Those were the ones used to celebrate the upcoming event days before the attack.

Now these potential pieces of evidences were inside paper bags, tagged, and ready to be sent to the laboratory. Along with the glasses, his entire office was inspected for fingerprints, and his computer and documents from the file cabinets were collected and carried to a 12-footer moving truck.

Gabriel and Hajak knocked the first pizza down and they were ready for the second one as they were watching the news and taking notes of the outcome as well as what law enforcement officials were doing, at least what was reported on television. It was announced that in an hour, the Governor of Florida was to give a press conference and that in three hours the President of the United States will address the nation with more knowledge from the preliminary investigation.

The FBI found out that all the latent prints on the glasses recovered from the professor's office at the university were not good for processing except one. They have identified the ones for Alfad Dal Kaden, a terrorist already wiped out from their list as intelligence reports informed of his death. The evidence was sent to Washington DC for a counterintelligence strategy and nothing was disclosed to anybody, to any agency, but to the head of homeland security, the head of the Central Intelligency Agency, the head of the National Security Agency, and the head of the Defense Intelligence Agency, as well as the President of the United States.

Alfad was brought up to live by the FBI counterterrorism team and they knew that this vital information could not be released to the press at anytime because it will alert and compromise the strategies to be taken against the forces of aversion. The Department of Homeland Security determined in their preliminary investigation that the terrorist attack was conducted by air, land, and sea combined with an almost perfect synchronization, and an almost undetectable and hard to predict participants. Two possible suspects were already on the charts at the Command Post, professor Sahkir and Alfad Dal Kaden. The press only knew about the professor possible involvement.

At 1600 hrs, Governor Rick Bresh was ready to address the public. He officially declared the Port of Tampa closed as a result of a terrorist attack and considering it as a crime scene, the biggest crime scene in Florida's history. The information released to the public was monitored by the Department of Homeland Security in which no specific terrorist group was yet identified. They limited their information to express their knowledge that the attack was indeed carry out by sea, land and air in conjunction with a meticulous monitoring terrorist plan and that federal agents were not able yet to process the scene until it was declared safe by the fire department. Rubble, smoke, dead bodies and dozens of wounded people was the catastrophic scene as television snapshots were aired from the news helicopters. The name of professor Sahkir was released since the press already knew about it without accusing him of his participation in the attack but to his presence in the airborne machine that collide with a combustible reservoir. No formal accusations were made. The public was informed that an exhaustive investigation still in process and that several calls have been received via the hotline generating multiple cases to be analyzed. The confirmation that forty-two dead bodies were recovered and that seventy-eight wounded people were treated on site, and sixteen other were medevac, was announced by the Governor.

Rick Bresh finished his press conference by indicating that at 18:00 hrs, the President of the United States will address the nation and maybe with little more information as the investigation evolves.

Hajak and Gabriel devoured the second pizza and concluded that no much outcome of the preliminary investigation was provided due to the fact that the scene was still unsafe for detectives to process it.

In the meantime, high-ranking official at the FBI headquarters in Washington DC, were cautious in handling Alfad Dal Kaden evidence and prepared a counterattack strategy to investigate how this individual entered the country and how he probably has left it. Hundreds of well trained FBI agents were assigned to sweep the entire city of Brandon and downtown Tampa targeting all hotels and motels, restaurants, which are the basic locations needed for survival and to recover video surveillance evidences if any to pinpoint Alfal Dal Kaden and to start establishing his presence, length of time before the attack, and about his comrades.

The American intelligence community didn't have any records of any kind of Alfad Dal Kaden leaving Iran since this was the place he last was reported alive. A national alert and manhunt was kept secret but every eye was put on Alfad as FBI agents were also targeting airports and car rental offices video surveillance.

The President of the United States was already addressing the nation when Hajak left the shower. Gabriel was taking notes. In Gabriel's mind, he was rewinding all memories to ensure that his real identity as Alfad Dal Kaden was perfectly covered. He knew that meticulous attention was given to places with cameras and that during his stay pretty much everything went well.

However, he also knew and accepted that perfection is something that does not belong to him but to the Almighty. He listened to the President and felt relaxed.

The President of the United States said nothing new. He indicated that the enormous list of tips was starting to make sense and taking shape, helping federal agents to investigate accordingly. He sent a message to the responsible party that there will be no rest from federal officers until it is determined who was responsible for the attack, its planning, and everything in relation to it and that the government of the United States will not negotiate ever with terrorists, and that they will be identified, apprehended, and brought up to justice. Hajak and Gabriel said at the same time: "Fuck you"!

The combatants were packing their stuff and getting ready to hit another motel to spend the night, maybe in the Daytona Beach area while still waiting for the Sheik's instructions.

They left the motel around 9pm and got into I-95 en route to Daytona Beach. They stopped in one of the rest areas on the highway to get some brochures for lodging; they were searching for a bed and breakfast type of location instead of a chain hotel where most likely cameras and a good registration system are in place. They found one, The Pleasant Waves Inn. Minutes after 11pm they arrived to the area but found the inn full of vehicles and lots of party goers, drove around the area and found another smaller inn with a hand-painted sign indicating vacancy. Hajak got out of the vehicle and knocked on the door. A middle age blonde lady answered the door and invited him inside. The lady showed him the living room with a big screen television set, down the hallway a French door that opens to the gardens and to the left of it another door that leads to the sandy beaches of the famous Daytona.

He directed his sight to the entire ceiling, walls, corners, and front desk area to ensure there were no cameras. He liked it and booked a room, maybe for the next three nights. He paid cash in advance, no receipts given and no ids requested; he just got the keys.

Hajak went outside to let Gabriel know where to park the vehicle and they both went to the room, a double-bed room with internet access. On the desk, a sign read: "Laptops for rent at the front desk". Gabriel went to the desk and got one, he was planning to log into the Aljazeera net to investigate about the incident. Hajak went to bed while Gabriel stayed until 01:50hrs browsing the net and collecting information about the investigation from several news websites.

A week has passed since the unfortunate event and it seemed that US officials were running out of time to respond to the demands from the public, the victims' families and the companies that were directly affected by the multiple blasts. FBI agents were working round the clock checking for video surveillance recording from several companies, to establish patterns, vehicles frequency, spotted drivers on cameras, adjacent locations, and any unusual circumstance that could call their attention. Another team of agents were recovering video surveillance from the port entrance to analyze all vehicles and persons that went inside the port that day.

After ten days of close forensic investigation, the very first finding that called their attention was the white van with the magnetic sign that read: "Atlantic Environmental Services", a group of forensic agents run a background check on this company and determined that no company existed with that name in the State of Florida. A national search indicated that were dozens of companies with that name and similar but with no business in Florida. Besides that, their logos, lettering, and colors were totally different.

By checking prior videos they targeted this vehicle and established a pattern of its visits and by matching the port authority log, they concluded that all entries were made to visit or to render services to American Python Company.

The terrorist plan included the destruction of the main building where officials from the Port Authority congregate to ensure the elimination of video surveillance archives. The Kaljatahl group did not have any knowledge that the daily recording of events was never sent to the local archives, it is saved and sent via the internet directly to the Captain of the Port alternate office on the federal building downtown Tampa, where all computer archives are kept. The FBI didn't know that either.

As soon as the information on the white van was confirmed, the FBI was in a desperate mood to say something to the American public. A press conference came as breaking news on national television and FBI officials and members of the Department of Homeland Security gathered together to announce their suspicions on the white van with the magnetic sign that read "Atlantic Environmental Services" that entered the port several times in the past two months to render services to American Python Company, services that were never received as informed by the company top executives. American Python Company was also involved in its own investigation but the inefficiency of its director of corporate security was not much of a help for local authorities. All the reports, logs, and paperwork related to vessel activities were not kept in records as instructed by the United States Coast Guard. This was the time when all the organisms, private and public have to work together and put in practice what is taught and mandated by the federal government. This was the time also for American Python to determine that the person they trusted their security was jerking off for several years and was dedicated to personal affairs instead of the needed security and that this person had no clue that sensitivity is priority and has no room for avoidance.

His ass was fired and the federal government was targeting the company as either voluntarily accessory to the execution of a terrorist attack or simple as a fuck up organization. They had to investigate and looked all the angles for possibilities.

Gabriel received the first call after breakfast while sitting on the garden reading the newspaper. Sheik Lazur almad Al Fanistar was worried about the breaking news in which government officials have identified a white van that may be in connection with the attacks. Gabriel was very upset and wanted to know what to do next. He never drove the van, so his image would not be on any video recording frame; however, Hajak's would.

Hundred of miles away inside a log cabin, a twenty-two year old man was enjoying his day off from work. He was playing with lego blocks with his five years old son while listening to the news at the same time. He stayed calm, stopped playing, and felt chilling sensations running up and down his short body. He just recognized Hajak from a video surveillance picture frame showed on television from the Port Authority video archives, and he had no doubts that he delivered two pizzas to a nasty motel to two individuals in room 125 ten days prior.

This man by the name of Scott immediately called the hotline number to report about Hajak. FBI agents were at his house in twenty minutes after the call. Four agents walked inside the living room and one of them stepped on the lego blocks on the floor where little Scottie was still playing. Scott was one hundred percent sure that the image he saw on television plus the enhanced picture they were showing him matched his recollection.

He didn't remember the name of the motel because it was a nasty place that didn't have any sign, but he volunteered to take them to the place. Scott ran to his neighbor's house to drop Scottie so she can watch the little boy while he was gone with the agents. An old, skinny, blonde lady by the name of Pat answered at the door. It was almost 10am and she already had alcohol breath but happy to take care of little Scottie. Scott advised the old bitch to watch the news just in case he is on it. She didn't understand a thing, but she sat on the couch anyway and was getting ready to roll and have some green stuff to smoke.

Upon arrival to the cheap motel, FBI agents interviewed the Pakistani owner who didn't carry any type of guest registration records. He wasn't even allowed to operate anymore since the city closed down his business for multiple code violations that were never taken care of. He thought he was in deep shit. In fact, he was. His ethnicity didn't help much either. Scott insisted that the pizzas were delivered to room 125. The owner of the establishment provided the keys to enter the room and stayed in the lobby while going under questioning by another agent.

Three FBI agents and Scott walked behind the little nasty establishment and stopped by a hand-painted door with the number 125. They were very careful when entering the room, it was partially clean, the bed was made, trash was dumped and fresh towels were in the bathroom. However, the owner confirmed that nobody has checked in into that room in the past twelve days. The FBI crime scene forensic team was called to process the room for fingerprints, and collection of any evidence such as fibers, hair, or anything that may help in the course of their investigation. Scott wanted to play detective; he was a daily viewer of Forensic Files on television. He went to the dump site and scream out loud: "Oh my God! the fuckin' boxes still here!".

He then ran back to the room and told the agents about it. The trash was removed from the room but not from the property. At this time, the crime scene became larger.

Fingerprints were lifted from all over the room and from the trash. The pizza boxes were recuperated and they still have written on it "Scott", the assigned delivery man from the pizza parlor.

The investigation case started to confirm and reconfirm that Alfad Dal Kaden was in town even after the terrorist attack and pointed out that most likely he was behind the masterminding of the attack, although the agents knew that the operative side is totally separated from the spiritually side, and that this one maybe took place somewhere in the world such as in Iran, Afghanistan, Syria, Iraq, or any other nation that harbors terrorists. It was time for Gabriel to go some place else and maybe to split from Hajak. It was necessary to reveal Alfad Dal Kaden's identity to get cooperation from the general public since authorities believed that this terrorist might still in town or at least in the United States.

Sheik Lazur almad Al Fanistar was aware of the worldwide manhunt for Alfad Dal Kaden. It was already broadcasted by the federal government. It has been fifteen days since American Airlines flight 1100 arrived in Turkey bringing aboard two members of the Kaljatahl group, Hassan and Kadu, and the same time for Delta airlines flight 256 that arrived in Frankfurt where Mardak and Wadek were staying. There was no communication among these pair of combatants.

In a secluded building near downtown Istanbul, Hassan and Kadu were ready to eat dinner at their friend's apartment. Izan Mawar was very happy to host these two combatants and at the dinner table they celebrated the triumph of the Kaljatahl group in Florida.

Izan has been living in Istanbul for the last seven years and he used to participate in several attacks against the Zionists in Israel. Their triumphant stories of each of the freedom fighters were shared throughout the evening. However in Germany, Mardak and Wadek were splitting; the first one will remain in Frankfurt and Wadek was leaving to Stuttgart. They both received a call from the Sheik and were ordered to remain in Germany pending notification to the next assignment either in London or elsewhere.

The FBI announced the presence of Alfad Dal Kaden in the United States and his name was put back in the systems of every intelligence agency. His fingerprints were lifted from the cognac glasses recovered from professor Sahkir's office at the university office; a fingerprint match was done from the pizza boxes recovered from the cheap motel, and he was also identified by Scott from a sketch that was released by the FBI.

The owner of the bed and breakfast where Hajak and Gabriel were staying in Daytona Beach was shopping at Walmart when she saw the sketches on the big screen television set in the electronics department. She couldn't believe that both terrorists were staying at her place. She almost collapsed and went back to her truck and drove straight to the police station to report them. Lieutenant Howard made contact with the FBI and a task force was immediately activated. Fifteen heavily armed officers from the SWAT team, about ten FBI agents and a dozen of police officers were en route to the bed and breakfast.
Hajak went to his room while Gabriel stayed by the pool area. Hajak needed a drink and got ready to go out and buy some alcohol. He entered the liquor store located about twelve blocks from the inn and on his way out he noticed a heavy police convoy going towards the inn area.

He knew it and there was nothing he could have done for Gabriel. The inn was surrounded by the SWAT team while police officers were stopping the traffic and served as the support team. When leaving the store, Hajak drove towards I-95 and started driving south not knowing where to go. He escaped from the clear and present danger.

Federal agents surrounded the inn without making any possible noise. A team of eight heavily armed police officers entered the establishment and they went directly to the back garden where Gabriel was lighting up the fifth Marlboro cigarette of the day. The heavy, firm, and fast steps of the gladiators dressed in black from head to toes were followed by a loud and constant shout: "Freeze, police, do not move"!! Gabriel was able to smell the end of the barrel of one of the officer's MP-5 pointed right at his face. He was immediately thrown to the ground, searched, and handcuffed. Several other officers went to the rented room in search for Hajak but they discovered that this one was not around. Crime scene personnel photographed the room and started to confiscate everything from the room. All possible evidences were bagged and tagged. Hajak was already about ten miles south on I-95.

Gabriel was interrogated but he was not cooperative with the authorities. He denied knowing where Hajak was. The police decided to remove the terrorist from the inn and transported him to the offices of the Department of Homeland Security located in Orlando, Florida, and placed many surveillance units in the area to wait for Hajak. The few guests from the inn were also interrogated and some valuable information was gathered. At the federal office, Gabriel was going under a scrutiny; fingerprints were collected and processed and compared with the national database managed by the Federal Bureau of Investigation. It didn't take that long to finally certify that Gabriel was in fact Alfad Dal Kaden. Hajak was about thirty miles south on I-95.

Federal agents and lab technicians were working hard and round the clock processing all evidences collected from the Port of Tampa. A month has passed since the coward attack and the first reports were already finalized. Certain video surveillance from restaurants, banks automated teller machines, gas stations, and port entrance showed Hajak's and professor Sahkir's faces as well as the white van holding the sign of Atlantic Environmental Services. Forensic investigators have mapped location, direction, and possible stops made with the white van by utilizing time framing, sequence and appearance between video frames to determine areas were they possible stayed. It paid off. They knew that the white van used to make left turns by the Shell gas station on Route 60 while driving on the east-bound side of the road right before I-75. This observation was an established pattern and close attention was dedicated to this particular area. After reviewing video surveillance archives from several lodging entities in the area, federal officials found out that the van used to go to the Red House Inn hotel in Brandon. Investigators determined that Hajak, Gabriel, and professor Sahkir were regulars. Also, after an extensive analysis of the property's documents and video surveillance it was established that other four individuals were detected in more than one opportunity. Federal officials were referring to Kadu, Hasan, Mardak, and Wadek, the Kaljatahl group. Hajak was very close to Port St. Lucie and he was in search for a mosque; he knew there was one in that town but he also knew that the feds were up his ass.

Alfad's cellular phone was analyzed by forensic investigators and a complete communication report was elaborated indicating incoming and outgoing calls, length of the calls, and text messages. Sheik Lazur almad Al Fanistar never called back. These two terrorists were abandoned in the United States.

Hajak made it to Port St. Lucie and stopped by a gas station hoping that the attendant at the 7-eleven can give him directions to the mosque. He was not that fortunate but the attendant told him the area where he should be looking for. Hajak was constantly thinking about Gabriel and felt super frustrated for not knowing what happened to him. The most difficult part was that they did not have communication at all. The reason why he looked for a mosque was to seek shelter, food, and the possibility to get assistance either to communicate with the Sheik or to fly out of the country. He found the mosque near the beach area and immediately parked his car without rolling the windows up. He ran to the door and entered in a rush stopping by the information desk. A heavy set gentleman took care of him and Hajak was taken into a room to be interviewed by a high ranking clergy. The man at the desk closed the main door and locked it not without peaking outside first. He lived in the premises and was ready for a drink before going to his secluded and spooky room for the night. Hajak remained inside the room and nobody has seen him yet.

Gabriel was inside a ten-by-four chilling concrete cell in Orlando and also thinking about what happened to Hajak, Did he get arrested also? Did he escape? Where is him? The cell door opened and he was transferred to an interrogation room where several homeland security officials were anxious to get more information about his whereabouts and the heinous attack.

Hajak was impatient and after twenty minutes of waiting, he wanted to go back to his car for a cigarette; he walked down the hallway but he was approached by a six feet tall man of tanned complexion, the leader of the mosque, Rashid Balak Ahmed. They went back to the spooky room to chat. Hajak explained the entire situation and asked for help to locate Sheik Lazur almad Al Fanistar in Afghanistan to let him know about Gabriel's arrest as to what to do next.

Rashid was not sure in getting involved on this matter since six months prior some federal agents were questioning him about Jared Balak Ranzi, his cousin under investigation for ties with some black men religious paramilitary organization based in Little Haiti, in Miami. These men were busted inside a warehouse where the feds confiscated high powerful rifles, ammunition, subversive propaganda, camouflage uniforms, and several other items and documents that might have a slightly connection with Al Q'aeda. Hajak needed some cash to rent a place somewhere in the vicinity; they both understood that it wasn't smart to stay together; however, Rashid was committed to locate the Sheik but with caution.

Both comrades went to the kitchen and got together to prepare something to eat for a late dinner. The television was on and the news was the only thing that appeared to be important. Fry fish and rice was ready in minutes, Rashid fried six fillets while Hajak volunteered to prepare a spinach salad with almonds, olive oil, red onions, and feta cheese. The men sat on a wooden picnic table inside the old kitchen room, the light was dimmed and the television volume lowered. Hajak had tears in his eyes lamenting the faith of Gabriel; he knew he was in jail and probably under severe interrogation. The feds already placed him at the scene of the terrorist attack and the could not let him go, he was the best asset but also the worst because he was not talking at all. When dinner was over, Rashid asked Hajak to wait while he was going to another room to get some cash. Minutes later the noise of the running water stopped, as Hajak who was doing the dishes noticed the report on the television set, one more time something new about the terrorist attack to the Port of Tampa. It was broadcasted that the feds had under arrest the most important element in the attack and labeled him as the mastermind and executioner of the entire plan, Alfad Dal-Kaden, a.k.a. Gabriel, who was already transferred from the offices of the Department of Homeland Security in Orlando to an undisclosed location characterized for its maximum security. But, the most chilling report was that Hajak's photograph was already made public and now he was under an extensive manhunt. Rashid entered the kitchen with some cash and missed the report in the news. He handled $425 to Hajak and asked him to leave the mosque after their prayers.

The prayers were intense and Hajak departed immediately after, not knowing where exactly to go and fearing for his life since he was already one of the FBI most wanted man. He went back to I-95 heading south and a couple hours later he found himself in Miami. He drove west on route 826 during the late hours of a Friday night ending on Okeechobee Road and started driving north on it. He found a motel in the industrial area of Medley and decided to rent a cheap room for the rest of the night. He was physically exhausted and mentally destroyed.

On Saturday morning, he went out to a nearby shopping center to use a public phone to call Rashid. It was already eleven o'clock and he couldn't believe how deep and long he slept. On the other side of the line Rashid gave him the good news. He had sent and email to several places in Afghanistan through an Islamic website, message that was sent strictly codified and that only leaders can understand it and able to disclose the real message. He was very confident that Sheik Lazur almad Al Fanistar will send a message back soon. Hajak was asked not to move from Miami yet and to remain in the industrial area. He went back to the motel and got glued to the television set for the entire day. He had previously purchased lots of junk food from vending machines, some sodas, and a newspaper.

In a secluded maximum security prison, agents from the ATF and FBI were discussing the presence of a great amount of C-4 utilized during the terrorist attack to the Port of Tampa and wanted to get some information from Alfad. The analysis showed that the explosive mass was not of American fabrication but instead it seemed to be from some kind of Russian mixed type. Several forensic analyses on the laptop used by Alfad while at the inn, showed communication with an individual by the fictitious name of Sebastian to an email address originated in Bali, but the email was sent to a server located in Caracas, Venezuela. The FBI and the Department of State had to deliberate the possibilities that the C-4 entered the United States as contraband from Venezuela. A couple of forensic studies on the laptop described the messages from Alfad to start making arrangements for more explosives for further attacks as plans were to be revealed by the Sheik, something that never happened since the Sheik suspended all types of communication with Alfad after his arrest.

Terrorist organizations are dependable groups on supplies, equipment and monetary distribution from foreign entities either directly or indirectly related to them, via governments that harbor terrorists or supporters of terrorism and through organisms dressed as non-profit organizations. At least, this is the case for Al

Q'aeda and Al Yamat terrorist organizations. The Kaljatahl group depended from outside help to gather, prepare, mount, camouflage, and transport all the explosives from the ranch to the port itself. One of the members, Hajak, knew that his faith was on the hands of the Sheik. He was even seeking the possibility of self-immolation in the name of the Almighty upon approval from the Sheik.

Rashid received an email from the Brothers of Islam for World Peace as an invitation (to see them) to pray and share the sacred messages (from the Sheik) and how to reach victory (how to leave the area). Under several codes, Rashid was able to understand that this non-profit organization made contact with the Sheik and that Rashid needed to go see them to receive the message from the Sheik. Telephone delivery was absolutely prohibited. The B.I.W.P. organization main center was located in Palm Beach County with similar annexes in Brooklyn, Seattle, and New Orleans. Rashid was very skeptical in going to Palm Beach to get the message and then deliver it to Hajak, he felt the steps of the feds behind him at all times and he was determined not to get in trouble.

Alfad Dal-Kaden was ready to be processed in a speedy trial; he was alone. The trial was to take place inside the prison with no access to the media and to the public. Three months have passed since the terrorist attack and the shouts for the death penalty for Alfad never quitted and he knew that there were no ways to escape from death.

Rashid grabbed a pack of cigarettes and got in the old Cutlass en route to West Palm Beach. An hour later he was there. He got out of the vehicle not without checking the area right and left to detect any movement of people or vehicles because he didn't want to be seized by the feds again. His walk was firm all the way to the building main door; he entered the multi-office building and walked straight to the elevators. While waiting for the elevator he took a peak to the directory board to make sure he was going to the right floor and to the right office. Seconds later, he was on the third floor right in front of an office with the initials BIWP on a plate besides the door. Somebody was waiting for him and the meeting was brief and straight to the point. A chubby middle age man opened the door and asked Rashid to enter the office, they talked behind the door and nobody sat or shared drinks. The chubby man stated: "Sheik Lazur almad Al Fanistar wants Hajak to go to this address in Miami", as he handled Rashid a piece of paper, and continued: "Hajak must be there by this weekend and wait for a telephone call from the Sheik himself". Rashid felt the rush as the chubby man opened the door inviting him to leave the office. Rashid left.

The same day, Rashid received a call from Hajak who still at the motel in the industrial side of Medley waiting for instructions. Rashid was on his way to the motel to deliver the instructions. Later on, the note was given to Hajak who read it and proceeded to pack all his stuff. The note indicated that at the address written on the paper was the place of residence of somebody by the name of Juan Martinez Ros, a Colombian-American drug dealer that will provide shelter for a couple of days. Martinez was the contact to obtain a fake English passport and the provider of $400 in cash and a flight ticket for Hajak from Miami to London.

Everything went as planned and as scheduled. Hajak was out of the United States of America under a fictitious name. The only terrorist left behind and the only one in prison was Alfad Dal-Kaden, but he was not talking.

For the next five years, and after his conviction and sentencing to life in prison without the possibility of parole in a maximum security prison, Alfad committed suicide by hanging himself while showering. He took with him to his death all the details and crucial information about the terrorist attack that paralyzed one of the most important and busy ports in the nation.

Are we really prepared to set in place effective anti-terrorism strategies? Are we really committed to a strong and efficient daily supervision of security operations? Are we still thinking that low trained and low waged private security personnel should be the main person to contact when trying to enter America's main doors? I don't think so............

The Port, Victor Guembes, USA, 2009